KT-133-854

Catherine Ryan Hyde is the author of several highly acclaimed novels including the award winning *Pay It Forward* (which was made into a feature film starring Kevin Spacey and Helen Hunt), *Love in the Present Tense* (a Richard & Judy Book Club bestseller), *Chasing Windmills*, *When I Found You*, *Second Hand Heart*, *Don't Let Me Go* and *The Hardest Part of Love*.

# Love in the Present Tense

Catherine Ryan Hyde

**BLACK SWAN**

TRANSWORLD PUBLISHERS
61–63 Uxbridge Road, London W5 5SA
a division of The Random House Group Ltd
www.booksattransworld.co.uk

**LOVE IN THE PRESENT TENSE**
**A BLACK SWAN BOOK: 9780552773645**

First published in Great Britain
in 2006 by Doubleday
a division of Transworld Publishers
Black Swan edition published 2007

Addresses for Random House Group Ltd companies outside the UK
can be found at: www.randomhouse.co.uk
The Random House Group Ltd Reg. No. 954009

The Random House Group Limited supports The Forest Stewardship
Council (FSC®), the leading international forest certification organisation.
Our books carrying the FSC label are printed on FSC® certified paper.
FSC is the only forest certification scheme endorsed by the leading
environmental organisations, including Greenpeace. Our
paper procurement policy can be found at
www.randomhouse.co.uk/environment

Typeset in 11.5/15.5 pt Bembo
by Falcon Oast Graphic Art Ltd.

Printed and bound in Great Britain by Clays Ltd, St Ives PLC

8 10 9 7

In memory of my friend

*Jody,*

a gentle man

whose love is

forever

## PEARL, *age* 13: **dying lessons**

One night when I was seven I watched a man die. He was on the street under my bedroom window. I was on my knees looking out. The sound, it had woke me. The window was open for air, which there was not much of, and what there was did not move. The curtain did not blow aside, and it was dark in my room, and I knew they could not see me.

The man who was going to die was on his knees. Like myself. Only with his arms out. Not up, like a stickup. Straight out, like Christ on his cross, only with his knees bent. I call him a man because I was only seven at the time. To me he looked big. Now I can remember his face, both before and after, and I know he was maybe sixteen. But I mistook him for a man.

The guys doing the killing, there were three, standing up. Laughing, which is what woke me I think. One of them had a sawed-off shotgun right in the man's face. Sort of a man. I guess if you are about to die like that, you're more than a boy.

Now the sort-of-man, he started to cry. Big crocodile tears. Or what they call that, anyway. Why they call them crocodile tears I don't know. I have never seen a crocodile cry. I have never seen a crocodile. But I watched a man die. So I know some things. Only maybe they are not the best things to know.

Then the almost-dead man, he started up begging. Please, he said. Please, think of my mama. Think of the kids I ain't even get to have yet. Please don't do this, I'll do anything, what do you want me to do? His shoulders shook, like a little earthquake right under the street that nobody could feel but him. His own little personal seven point one, just under his knees.

Please, he said, and the one with the sawed-off shotgun shot him in the face. Then the three, they walked off laughing. Turned the corner, laughing. I had to keep watching, because I was afraid to not watch. I was afraid to go back to bed. Because the dead sort-of-man, he would still be there. He had to be where I could see. I remember real good what he looked like after, but it's something I do not plan to say a whole lot about. Because some things, they are plain ugly. This thing, I figure it's bad enough *I* know.

After a while the cops came, and I got tired, and they were there to look and know where he was, so I went back to bed.

There is no mercy. Give up on that. Don't ask.

I decided when my number came up someday, I would not beg. I would take my dignity with me. They say you can't take it with you, but mostly about money and cars and such. Dignity, I think you can. And I think you will miss it sorely if you leave it behind. Anyway, we all believe what we want and that's what I believe.

Speaking of dignity, it is dignity when you own what you did. Not pretend. So, I shot that man. Just like they think I did. I will say that now. I shot that man between the eyes, in Rosalita's kitchen, where he stood with no pants on. Killed him with his own gun. It was my birthday that day. I was thirteen.

I knew he was a cop, but what difference is that supposed to make? Even if I could have known somehow I would die for it later. It's always better to die later. A time like that, you have to make a fast choice, and it's never die/not die. It's always die now/die later. Rosalita taught me that. She said, "Girl, comes clear somebody's number 'bout to be up, try and see it ain't you. Let him die now, you die some other time. When your number finally come up, you'll be ready. You'll've had lotsa practice." That made sense to me. But I don't think that's why I shot him.

I did not laugh or have fun.

I guess I felt some bad for it later, but at the time I don't know what I felt. Not the half of what I should've, that I can say for a fact. I was not a cold person. Just alive, like everybody else, and trying to stay that way awhile longer.

I guess I felt bad later because I could've let go of the gun. Not pulled on it. I think if I'd just let him take it back he might not've hurt me or anything. But then you don't know for a fact and you just do something and then it's the wrong something. I worry sometimes, did I shoot him because he didn't love me and never would? But I really think it wasn't on purpose. Only, sometimes I see people fool themselves, so I ask myself all the same. But I don't think I meant for it to happen. Besides, if I was to kill everybody who didn't love me and never would, wouldn't be nobody left on the planet but maybe Rosalita and Leonard, my little boy. Who, of course, was not even borned at the time.

This is how it was.

On account of it was my birthday, I had been almost all day looking for Mama. What one of these things has to do with the other I can't say that I know. What I thought she would do about it being my birthday, well, she wouldn't do nothing. That much is real clear now. But it made me look for her all the same.

To make things worse, Rosalita had got arrested, only this time she did not come back. And I had to wonder why. Usually it wouldn't take her no more than two, three hours to make it home. Cop would pick her up, take her on a ride supposed to be to the station. Only they'd go someplace else, she doing for him for free what he was supposed to be taking her in for. Then he'd drop her back on the corner.

This time she did not come home all day. Maybe some cop really put her in jail. Maybe he didn't want nothing from her, or had kids and a wife he wanted to stay true to for real. Or a bag of other maybes I could not understand. What had happened to things? I didn't know.

I went by to where Little Julius was sitting out on his stoop and I asked him did he see my mama.

"Maybe I seen her," he said. "Maybe I ain't. Why'nt you come over a little closer here and we talk about it?"

I didn't get no closer to Little Julius. He was a big fat man with his hair shaved all off and little designs shaved in, and, when he smiled, his front teeth were all gold. You would think it would look nice—all that gold. But no. It was ugly in a way I could never explain. He liked the color of my skin because of me being part black and part Korean. He said I am fine. Not that day, but he had said it. In the past. And even that day, even with him not saying it, you could feel that hanging around.

I said, "Maybe did you sell her something?"

Little Julius said, "Ain't got nothin' to sell. Ain't got no product. If you would listen to reason maybe I would have. You and me, we could do okay. Little girl like you, just don't have no idea what you got. You and your mama, live in a real house. You'd be doin' okay."

I knew we were talking two very different kinds of

things and so did he. I cared and Little Julius, he did not.

"Who she buy from when she don't buy from you?"

Little Julius frowned. Frown like that means maybe time to back up. Maybe time to get the hell somewhere else.

I say no to guys all the time. Every day. Most don't like it any too much. Sometime I say yes. The good ones, they're not sure what they feel. Feel too many things at once. They are the only kind I say yes to. The too-sure kind, I say no. They got no conscience to make them feel some other things. Watch out for that.

I waited under the freeway overpass for some guy they called Slacker. Listening to the cars go over my head—thump-thump, thump-thump—I was wondering what makes that thump sound. If there are bumps in the road or something. But I never been on that road, or most others. Me and Mama didn't have a car. I was wondering should I go back in and ask for this Slacker guy again. But I was in that bar once already, and the bartender man, he threw me out. Said I would lose him his license. Said he would send this Slacker out to see me.

Thump-thump. How long it would take him to come out and see me I didn't know.

I was thinking maybe I would just go on back to Rosalita's. Give this up for the day. But it's a long walk back there. If I had bus fare maybe I would've already been gone. The day was already almost over.

Then this man came walking by. Looked too good to be down there. You know, with a suit and all. A white man with a shiny gold wedding ring. I was sitting on the sidewalk and he looked down at me and I looked up at him, and I knew he had the taste. I could see it in his eyes. And I knew he would give me some money if I asked, because he did not know it. At least, he did not know it out loud. So he would think he was looking at me for some much nicer reasons. Like I am this nice young person he wants to help out, and like there is no shame in a thing like that. I looked up into his eyes like I had fallen into something I couldn't quite find my way out of. Which in some ways was the truth.

"You okay?" he said.

"Can't get home," I said. "No bus fare."

He took out his wallet and pulled out three one-dollar bills. I could tell he did not ever ride the bus and was trying to think what that might cost. I didn't tell him, because then he would give me the most he thought it might be. He reached it down to me and I wondered what he would do if my hand touched his when I took it. I knew he was a man who would feel lots of things at once. I could say yes to a man like that. Maybe get a steak dinner for my birthday. But then he let go real quick and walked on. I watched his back walking away. That is a man who knows trouble when he scrapes by it.

That's what I told myself while I watched him walk away.

Then next thing I knew this white dude with his hair slicked back came out of the bar and said maybe he is Slacker and maybe not. All depends on who is asking. I said I am asking and then he figured maybe yeah, that's who he is.

I asked him did he see my mama. And I told him about the scar she wore on her face, so that way he would know which mama she is.

He said yeah, maybe he might've made a sale to a person such as that, and maybe by now she would've gone on home to use up what she got. Like that answered everything, he said that to me, and stared me down. And I said shoot, Mr. Slacker, we don't live noplace. Like what was he thinking? Used to we had a real apartment, but that's been a long time now.

He just shook his head and went back inside the bar.

I stood a minute more under that overpass. Thump-thump. Thump-thump.

Then I walked to the bus stop, thinking it was good I had three dollars.

Before I could even get there this boy slapped me up against the brick of a place. No one around to see. Boy no older than me. Younger maybe. But bigger. Held me there with his dirty self that smelled bad.

"What you got for me?" he said. "Got any money?"

I thought for a minute about that three dollars, and would I fight for it. I can take an ass whipping. I done so many times. But it was my birthday and also I could not see getting my ass beat for three dollars. That white man with the shiny gold ring, where was he now when I needed him?

"I got three dollars," I said.

"Shit, that ain't no money," he said.

So I said, "Fine. Don't take it then."

But he did take it. Stuck his hand deep down in the pocket of my shorts and took it away and then pressed his dirty self up even closer and said he can take what he wants. I was just about to spit on his face.

But then he said, "Don't want nothing from you, though."

And he let me go. I spit on him just the same, and he kicked me in the leg and ran away.

I sat on the bus bench anyway, because sometimes there is this one driver on this route who will let me ride even if I don't pay. He puts a finger to his lips and real quiet says, I got to go there anyway, don't I now? With you or without you. He is nice. But a bus came by and it was not him driving. It was this lady. She stopped and put the door open with that noise sounds like an old man complaining while he sits down. She looked at me and I looked back.

"Getting on?" she said. "Don't have all day."

"No money," I said. And she closed that door and rolled away.

It was starting to get dark. I'd been sitting on that bench a real long time.

I knew there was one more place to look for Mama, but it was a long walk and not someplace I really so much wanted to go. I was thinking maybe I did not need to find her quite that bad.

Then the cop car stopped for me.

So much of how it was started when that cop got out and came up to me. But I didn't know all this when it first happened. I guess you never do. I didn't know there would ever be a Leonard, or that this man would be his father, or that anybody would have to die. I didn't know where all this would take me at the time.

This cop, he got down on one knee by the bus bench. "You been sitting here an awful long time," he said. "You been letting some buses go by. You got a way to get back home?"

I looked at his badge, and his little name thing. It said Officer Leonard DiMitri. I looked past him to his partner waiting in the car. His partner had a mustache and his lip was funny underneath. Like one of those lips start out in two pieces, and later the guy grows a mustache to cover it but you can still see where the split was. He had this look like he didn't like what was starting up here. Maybe it was just the lip but I don't think so. Then I looked back at Officer Leonard, right up into his face, and I smiled back at him, and I saw he had the taste. And I thought, good. Now I can get back to Rosalita's place, and finally this day can be over.

I got in that car with them and he asked me my name,

and I told him. First and last both. Right in front of that lip man. I don't know why. I had got happy and forgot to be careful. It was stupid, I knew right away. How stupid, well. I had to wait to know that.

First thing he said—this Officer Leonard, when he saw Rosalita's place—he said, "My oh my. Your mother certainly keeps this place awfully clean."

I did not tell him Rosalita was not my mother. I did not tell him that I was the one who kept that place so clean. Clean, that is a big thing with me. When I live someplace you can eat off the floor in that place. Off the seat of your chair. Right out the stainless steel sink. There will not be one germ. Not if I have my way. Every place I go, I make that place clean. Turns out that is a good thing, because when you make places clean wherever you go, seems you always have someplace you are welcome. I was trying to decide what to tell Officer Leonard and what to not tell.

He had dropped his partner with the lip back at the station, end of shift, and then turned in his patrol car, and then he had drove me back to Rosalita's in his own car, which was this Corvette with the T-roof and all. Man did I like riding in that car. It was like a whole birthday all by itself. Just before we drove off, his partner, the guy with that weird lip, he gave Officer Leonard a funny look and said something I could not hear. But my friend Leonard, my birthday man, he waved it off like he knew just what he was doing.

"Come upstairs," I said when he got me back to what I sort of called home.

He didn't ask any questions or anything. In fact we was both real quiet until we got upstairs and he said that thing about the clean.

I took his hand and pulled him at Rosalita's bedroom. He said one more thing. He said, "Are you sure? Are you sure this is what you want?" This is something a man will say when he's feeling a lot of things at once. When he's not the kind of man who would do this if he thought you might not be sure. But I was surprised because we both knew right on that bus bench and it seemed kind of funny to stop to talk about it now. But I was glad that he did. All the same.

He was a big tall man and I think he was Italian. Anyway, he was handsome, with wavy dark hair. He did not have a gold wedding ring but sometimes a guy will be married without one. I wondered if he was married. If he had a kid my age. Even so, I was thinking he might love me. Then things would all change, right from that day on. Even if he was married. Rosalita had a man once who loved her. He was married but he paid her rent and came over three times a week and brought flowers and wine. I thought maybe this was my birthday present. Someone who would love me and pay the rent. I never answered that question he asked. We didn't say nothing more for a long time.

★ ★ ★

Way later he said another thing to me and it made me laugh. He said, "I never did something like this before." He said it in this mushy voice from deep inside his chest. He had a hairy chest. Talking so deep inside it, that made me think even more that maybe he would love me.

"What?" I said. "You never did sex before? I can't believe that." I said. "Now don't start lying to me, just when everything was going so good."

"No, not that," he said. "That's not what I meant. Sex, yeah. Just not with somebody, you know. Your age."

Maybe he was lying about that. I've wondered lots of times. I think about that a lot, was that a lie or was it the truth? Did he really want a younger girl all those years and not do that? Or was that just something you say? A lot of what I have heard in my life was lies. So I really wondered about that. Looking back, it seems a shame that I killed him when I did, and now there's no way I ever get to find out.

After that he got kind of funny and young, like he wanted to play. He even tickled me some, like I was a kid, only we were naked in Rosalita's bed. No place for a kid there. Then he got real serious and brushed the hair off my face and looked me right in my eyes. "I'm so glad I met you." That's what he said. Right into my eyes, he said that.

And I thought, this is how love feels. I know that now. Happy birthday to me.

Then he looked over my shoulder and there was a clock back there. "Shit," he said. "I gotta go. I gotta get home. Shit."

That feeling, that thing I thought was love, I just watched it blow away. I thought, you spend so much time looking for it but then it blows away so fast. I wished I had known.

I got up and walked into the kitchen. Rosalita's very clean kitchen. I was feeling bad because I knew I was wrong about the love. He was getting dressed to go away and he wasn't never going to come back with any flowers or wine. He was just looking for something to do for that night only. If that's love, you can keep it.

I was starting to get mad.

His uniform jacket was hanging over the kitchen chair. Under it was the big belt with his gun. I was holding his pants on account of I'd picked them up off the bedroom floor. I was folding them neat to hang up. All I was going to do was hang them up with his jacket. My thought was never to steal nor to kill nobody. It was not supposed to come down like that. Maybe I just took the pants because I hate things to be lying around the floor. Or maybe I wanted him not to be so fast to go. But then there was his wallet. I could feel the lump in his pocket.

Usually I would never take something. I'm not a killer nor a thief. But I was mad at him and I thought I should take enough to buy a birthday present, since he was not it, like I thought.

He came out in the kitchen with no pants on and looked at me funny. "You need money?" he said. "Just ask. I'll give you a few bucks."

I guess he meant it nice. Looking back I think maybe he meant it nice. But at the time I thought he was catching me as a thief and calling me a whore in the bargain. I am not a whore. What I do I do either for love or what I think might be love. If I am wrong, I am wrong, but I am no whore.

He was walking at me so I took up his gun.

I guess I thought, he has caught me stealing. I'm in trouble now. I pointed the gun at him. It was heavy and big. This all happened really fast. He still had this sweet look on his face, only now he looked sweet but also worried. Scared. Like I might really shoot him. But I never thought I would. But I flipped the lever that lets the gun really shoot, to make him think I would. I was just saying keep away.

But then he reached out fast like lightning and grabbed my hand. The one that had the gun. And it hurt, because it made the metal of the gun press too hard on the bones in my hand. So I pulled really hard, to get my hand and the gun back again. Just to make sure if he got it he wouldn't be mad and use it on me. I was afraid to let him take it. And then there was a big sound. It scared the life out of me, but at first I didn't even know it was the gun going off. I don't know why it went off. I guess when I pulled my hand back I squeezed too hard, but I don't know. It happened fast. Like I said.

Then I was all surprised, because I shot him. I didn't know that was about to happen. Also I was surprised when that little spot came up between his eyes. I thought the gun was aimed straight, at his belly. I guess when I pulled my hand back I pointed it up. Or maybe he was trying to point my hand up so I wouldn't shoot him. Which I never thought I would do. But I don't really know what happened. Just that it all happened fast.

I thought all these different things at once. I thought, that did not make a mess at all. I thought it would make a mess. Then he crumpled down with that same look on his face and I saw the curtains behind, and what was on them. I thought, oh, shit. This place will never get clean, never again. I thought, this is bad, what happened. I thought, Rosalita won't let me live here anymore. I looked down at his face and he still had that sweet look on his face. I thought, what if he really did love me?

I took his credit cards and his money and his gun.

And I went to look for Mama in that last, awful place.

I found her there, too. It was this house, this boarded-up house. But I knew how to get in the back. The people there are terrible but they will not do you no harm. They are too loaded to care. Mama was in the kitchen, leaned up on this stove that something had dripped all down. Like spaghetti sauce that nobody bothered to clean. How can people live like that?

"Hi, Baby," she said, but the words kind of ran together and her chin nodded around.

There was no place clean I could go. Rosalita's would never be clean and this place neither. But I wanted to stay with Mama now that I had found her. I was feeling strange.

I went down to the corner store and bought a roll of paper towels and that kind of cleaner you spray from a plastic bottle. With the money out of Officer Leonard's wallet. Some of it anyway. I took it back to that awful house and made a clean spot on the kitchen floor near her.

Then I felt better, on account of I was cleaning. I did not want to think too much but I thought real simple things. I thought in the morning I would go see Little Julius and sell him the credit cards and the gun. By thinking things like that I did not think too much else.

Mama passed out before it was clean. So I took her by her coat and I pulled her over into my clean place and I lay beside her. Lay down in the clean and tried to get some sleep. I can't sleep if it isn't clean. I tried not to think about what was right outside that little circle of clean.

I had a baby in me. Just as of that night. Just that night it had happened, and I knew it.

Now, in the time that passed between then and now I have told that to a few people. They said I am crazy and I am wrong. They said you can't know that so soon. They said if a woman could know that so soon they wouldn't sell the little tests you pee on. She would just know. I don't care what they say. I knew there was a baby in me, and I knew a baby is somebody who would always love me. Forever love, that's what you get from a baby. He does not look at the clock and say oh shit. I better go home.

I made up my mind I would love him forever right back. That would be my whole job in the world.

So, that was my present. After all.

I went to sleep with my head on Mama's coat.

MITCH, *age 25:* **phone calls from the top**

I was in a singularly bad mood that morning. I was standing in the middle of the goddamn street trying to flag down the FedEx truck, because my faithful so-called employees had forgotten to arrange the pickup. I was standing there waving my arms like a jackass in the middle of the goddamn street. I don't know if the FedEx guy didn't see me or just pretended he didn't. But he swung around the corner and he was gone; one way or the other, I was pissed.

I was thinking, fire somebody. I have got to fire somebody. This is no way to run a fucking business. I was thinking, this is why you shouldn't hire your friends. Because you can't bring yourself to can their asses in a pinch. I was thinking, you start a business out of your home, they forget this is real. Think it's a game. Not to me it isn't.

Then I heard this voice, this funny little voice. "Hello, down there." I looked around. It was weird. If it was one of my people playing a joke, it wasn't so goddamn funny. I was in no mood. "Up here," it said.

"Who is that?" I said.

"It's me. Leonard."

"Leonard who?"

"Leonard up here."

I looked up at the second-floor window of the house next door, and there was this little kid waving to me. Like he thought I was waving my arms at him, so he was waving back. I didn't have the heart to tell him how wrong he was, and all that rage just slipped out of me even though I needed it to stay.

I walked over until I was standing in the grass under his window. "Hello up there," I said.

"Hello down there," he said.

He was kind of Asian looking, somewhat. Kind of melting pot multiracial I guess. He smiled, and his front teeth weren't all the way grown in. He had this dark, really jet-black hair that was noticeably unruly. It stuck up on his head like a spiky little weed patch. Shiny, like somebody had been trying to slick it down unsuccessfully. I was trying to remember what I'd just been all pissed off about because right at that moment I thought I still wanted it back.

"Leonard what?" I said.

"Leonard Leonard. Just Leonard. That's all the name there is."

I figured he was playing a game with me, but it was an okay game, really, far superior to what waited for me back inside. "That's the whole name, huh? Just Leonard?"

"Yuh," he said. He was wearing these really thick Coke-bottle glasses with heavy black frames, and the way he was leaning out the window, I was positive they were about to fall into the grass at my feet.

"You're going to lose those glasses," I said.

"No way. Look." He turned his head over so he was nearly looking at the sky, and I could see a wide black elastic band holding them in place.

"Pretty cool," I said.

"Yuh," Leonard said. "I know."

When I got back inside, Cahill was holding the phone receiver for my private line. "For you, Doc," he said. With this funny look on his face.

"Don't tell me, let me guess. It's a little kid."

"Right you are, Doc." He seemed to feel better, knowing all this at least made sense to me.

I took the phone. "Leonard," I said, tucking the receiver between my shoulder and chin.

"Hi, Mitch. It worked."

"You did good, Leonard." I sat down at my computer and settled back to the task in front of me, sorting through a slough of HTML code on a Realtor's Web site, to see

27

why we were getting complaints about bad links. They looked okay to Graff, which wasn't saying much for them.

"What should we talk about?" he asked.

"I don't know. What do you talk about when you call total strangers?"

"I dunno," he said. "Stuff."

I was feeling distinctly less like canning somebody. "Okay. Talk to me about stuff."

Oh boy did he. For nearly an hour. All kinds of stuff. He talked about moon races on the way up from L.A. and borrowed cars with the keys left in. The race came out a tie and by the way he was five years old. And a lady named Rosalita who he thought was his grandmother but really it turned out he didn't have any, and how they visited Rosalita in jail. He told me he got "borned" too soon, and that his mom's name was Pearl and she left L.A. with him because she thought they'd be safer here, and that he didn't have a last name. And that he had to spend tons and tons of time at the clinic. He told me it was really clean over there because his mom liked it that way, and that Mrs. Morales who owned the house liked the way Pearl kept it clean, only now Pearl was out at somebody else's house, cleaning over there, too, and Mrs. Morales was supposed to look in on him every few minutes to see he was okay, but then she fell asleep in front of the TV and never did. He said when he got big he was going to get a great big dog like the one that gets walked down this street every day at six in the morning; did I ever see that dog?

28

"Six a.m.," I said. "I am *always* snoring at six a.m." And he laughed.

Then he told me a lot more stuff.

After I got off the phone I looked up and Cahill was staring at me. "What was all that about?"

"Oh, that kid next door."

"There's a kid next door?"

"I didn't know it either until just now."

"How'd he get your private number?"

"I read it off to him while we were talking just now. We were talking out his window. I had him dial it right then while I was reading it off to him. Then I taught him how to hit redial."

Cahill just stared at me for a minute. He was even younger than me, and I was only twenty-five at the time. He had one of those haircuts shaved on the sides but long on top. That morning he had this mean cowlick near the back. He was definitely having a bad hair day. "*Why?*" he said.

"Shit, I don't know, Cahill. Why not? He's over there all by himself. Dialing up total strangers. If he's going to talk to a total stranger, I figured it should be me."

Cahill had a big mental filing cabinet of my eccentricity and unreasonableness. I watched him silently file this new evidence away.

★　★　★

Ten o'clock that night the phone rattled me out of sleep. I don't usually go to bed nearly so early but I'd gotten only two hours the night before. It's a long story.

My first thought and my fondest wish was Barb, but I halfway expected it to be Leonard. If it had been, it would have been call number five for that first day. It was a girl. A young girl. Not Leonard young, but young. Teenage.

"Who is this?" she said.

"No," I said. "No, that won't cut it. You called *me*. You tell me who *you* are." I hate it when people do that. Doesn't anybody know phone etiquette anymore?

"Why's my son been calling this number? I hit the redial, see who he's been calling. Who the hell are you?"

"I live right next door," I said. My voice softened a little. I couldn't help it. It was kind of touching. It was what I wanted. Some proof this kid had a real momma lion on patrol for him. I told her, "If you were in the back room and my blinds were open we'd be watching each other make this call." I was in my loft, upstairs. The whole downstairs had pretty much become the business.

"Why's he been calling you?"

"Because I gave him this number. He was calling total strangers."

"He still is," she said. "You're a total stranger. To me." Her voice hadn't softened yet.

"My name is Mitch," I said. "Sometimes people call me Doc, though."

"Why? You a doctor?"

LOVE IN THE PRESENT TENSE

"No. It's just a joke. My initials are M.D." No response. "It's a joke."

"I don't get that joke."

I sat up in bed. Reached over to pull up the blinds, but I reached over so far I almost fell off the bed. But I got the blinds up. I wanted to see her. She sounded so young. Maybe fifteen or sixteen. Maybe she was a lot older but just had a little-girl voice. I wanted to see who I was talking to. But all I saw was a glow behind white curtains. "You know," I said. "That woman you rent from . . . I know you think she looks in on him while you're gone. But she doesn't."

I waited a long time, but the line just went quiet. Then I heard a little sound. Might have been a sigh, or she might have been crying. I couldn't tell.

"I don't know what I'm supposed to do," she said. "I gotta work."

"What's your name?" Leonard had told me but I couldn't remember.

Barb always said I'm born to pick up strays. But Barb was not there. Then again, when was Barb ever there? If she had been available I might have told her that she should come around more often. Maybe I wouldn't need the strays. She wasn't around to hear that pointed complaint, though, which was the point.

"Pearl."

"Pearl what?"

"Pearl none of your business. Pearl's all you need to know."

31

"Why don't you try dropping him here while you're gone?"

"Oh, sure. With you. Great. How do I know you don't molest little boys?"

"Because . . . I don't."

"Good answer," she said. "You should run for politics."

"Look, I'm not the only one here," I said. "There are four of us, minimum. All day. We're working here. Doing software and Web design and stuff like that. He's not going to be alone with anybody. He's safer here, believe me. He's going to fall right out that window one of these days."

I waited a long time for her to answer. I thought she was just taking her time. I never heard her hang up the phone. Until I heard that dial tone I didn't realize she had.

Twenty minutes after nine the following morning, I got a knock on the door. All of us were hard at work. Well, not all of us. Hannah and Cahill and me. Graff hadn't found his way in yet. When did Graff ever fall in before ten a.m.? He's the one I should've canned. Only he's not the one who blew the FedEx pickup; that was Hannah. And I couldn't fire her because she thought the sun rose and set on me. She'd have never been the same.

"Come in," I said without getting up. But nobody did. "Come in." I said it louder this time. All of our customers—that is, the very few who care to drop by in person—know enough to just barge through the door. I was thinking, goddamn Jehovah's Witnesses. I was thinking one of these days I'd have to tie those suckers up or hold a gun to their heads and make them listen to my views for a change. See how they liked it.

I blasted out of my chair and over to the door. Threw it open. I was pissed.

On my doorstep was this little girl. Maybe sixteen years old. Or maybe as young as fifteen or as old as seventeen or eighteen. Maybe part black but definitely Asian, with the sweetest, deepest dark eyes. She was one seriously beautiful little girl. Hanging off one of her hands was the irrepressible Leonard.

I thought, this could not be Leonard's mother. No way. Unless she had him when she was like, twelve. That's not possible. Is it?

"Pearl?" I said.

"Maybe Leonard could stay here today. I'm still thinking."

She walked past me and looked the place up and down. Both Hannah and Cahill fell out of their seats and fell into line, like some kind of military inspection. Pearl inspired that. I introduced them both, but Pearl didn't offer her hand to shake or anything. Just looked up at them like she was taking mental notes. Pearl was very small.

Meanwhile Cahill was giving me this look and I knew he was filing this as further evidence against me.

I introduced Leonard to the Avian Americans, as Cahill

liked to call them. I had these two big cockatoos. A rosy Moluccan and a pure white. Pebbles and Zonker. I explained to Leonard with great care that Zonker was very nice and friendly but Pebbles had to be avoided at all costs. And I color-coded them for him. White good. Pink bad.

"Why is she bad?" he wanted to know.

"She bites," I said.

"Hard?"

"Very hard. She has a beak that can crack walnuts." He didn't seem impressed. "Know what a walnut is?"

"Like a peanut?"

"No, much harder. She could break one of your little fingers."

"Ouch," he said.

I took Zonk down off the cage and he hopped rather eagerly onto Leonard's head and preened at little bits of his spiky weed-hair, causing the kid to positively shriek with laughter and delight.

"Okay," Pearl said. "He can stay here. I've decided it's okay."

She moved toward the door. Cahill gave me this snooty look, this kind of sarcastic thank-God-we-passed-muster thing. She was rude, there was no arguing that. No defending her.

"Leonard," she said. "Got your inhaler?"

"Check," he said, patting his shirt pocket. His shoulders popped up around his ears, like that would somehow make his head, with its big overwhelming bird ornament, disappear.

I took Zonker onto my fingers, put him back up on the cage.

Pearl stopped at the door and looked over her shoulder at me. Such a tiny, fragile beauty. "Mr. Doc," she said. "Thank you. This is very nice."

And she left before she could see how stunned I was to hear it.

Not ten minutes later Leonard stuck his hand out to the wrong bird and got it bitten. I was in the kitchen area starting a third pot of coffee. The shriek brought every-body running. Even Graff, who had managed to get his sorry ass into work by then.

Leonard held his little damaged finger up for me to see. It wasn't broken. Actually it hadn't even broken the skin. But there was a definite red mark.

"Go get him some ice," I told Hannah. I was feeling a little better about Pebbles, because I knew that had not been her best shot. She had cut the poor kid a moment's slack.

"Remember what I told you about Pebbles?" I said, wiping off his tears with the paper towel Hannah brought us and applying the ice, which made him wince.

"Yuh. You said she'd crack me like a nut."

"Right. She's the rosy one."

"What's rosy?"

"Pink."

"Yuh," he said. "I know."

He was just a kid. Five years old. He swore he understood the difference between the two birds but I was sure he had simply transposed the names, descriptions, and reputations.

It never occurred to me at the time that even with those big thick glasses he couldn't see well enough to tell the two apart.

## LEONARD, *age* 17: **photo, last name, father**

I have no photos of Pearl. Not one. At least, none that survived her leaving.

I have a strong memory of her, a mental picture of her face, looking down on me with love. From the minute I was born, I think. She believed in looking down on her baby, me, with a face full of joy. Welcoming, she said. She said we should all be welcomed into the world with joy. I remember her telling this at length to Rosalita, who I used to think was my grandmother, when we went to visit her. Turns out she wasn't, though. So, grandparents. Another thing I don't have. I should add that to the list.

Thing is, because I have no photo, I can no longer picture her face. I still see and feel her looking down on me with love, but I can't re-create that Pearl face, that sweet child. So now all I see is the love. Which, actually, is not such a bad deal. You could do a lot worse.

Every young man thinks his mother is an angel. The Madonna, beyond reproach. And I guess I'm no exception.

But there are two things I wanted from her and never got. Two things I begged her to tell me but she never did. I wanted to know who my father was. And I wanted to know my last name.

Better not to know, she said. Trust me on this, she said.

I wanted to trust her. I meant to. But then instead I memorized the name she gave when she took me to the clinic. I couldn't help it. Said it over and over so I wouldn't forget. But I didn't know how to spell it. I could only sound it out in my head. It was like, Dim . . . eat . . . tree.

I learned it just in time for her to tell me: Forget it. It isn't ours anyway.

She was scared of something. I wonder sometimes if what she was scared of is what got her in the end. It doesn't always work that way, you know. Sometimes we think we know what to fear. We never turn our back on it. Then something else we never thought of comes along. I wonder if what finally caught her in the end was something she feared all that time, or something she never would have thought of.

I'm thinking all this as I work on the hang glider in the half-dark. I'm working by candlelight. Because what I'm doing, it's this taping thing. I went out and bought ten rolls of duct tape. Sounds crazier than it is. The duct tape doesn't have to hold it all together. The fabric is also sewn.

The tape just seals flat all the fabric edges so the wind can't get underneath.

I was told you can also use wax, but I couldn't bring myself to do it. I kept thinking about Icarus, flying too close to the sun. I don't know how close I might get. I don't want to commit.

While I'm feeling the tape under my fingers, smoothing it down, feeling each edge adhere to the fabric, taut and perfect, I'm thinking about the last time I saw Pearl. The way she grabbed hold of my arm and yanked me down the street toward Mitch's house. Very sudden. I knew she had seen something, but I didn't look around. I was only five. I never got to see what she saw. I think about that a lot now. I had a chance to see the devil, the bogeyman, but I didn't look over my shoulder. I was just thinking about getting to Mitch's house. Wondering if he got that new computer game he promised me. I didn't know it was an important moment. I guess you never do.

Now Jake comes in and sits in the garage with me. "Hey," he says.

"Hey," I say back.

"You're crazy," he says.

"We been through this before."

"No, I mean, turn on the light."

"Don't need the light. This is something I'm better to do by feel."

It's like blindness, a subject I feel qualified to speak about. It turns up my sense of touch. I am feeling tautness, smoothness. I am better off, just in this moment, without my eyes.

The candlelight throws a great huge shadow of the bird craft onto the rafters of the garage. It's breathtaking, really. The aluminum frame is covered with fabric now, but the candlelight bleeds through it like an X-ray, stripping it bare and showing its bones. It's almost a religious thing. To look at, I mean. I think even Jake is filled with a certain reverence.

Now I'm thinking about Pearl coming into the hospital to hold me when I was all tiny and premature. I don't know how prematurely I was born but I get a sense from her stories that it was a big deal. I'm thinking about how she fought the nurses for the right to look down at me with that welcoming love. There were visiting hours, but she more or less told them to kiss her ass. Not that I remember this exactly but I remember being told. And I believe I have some trace memory of that beam of welcoming love.

Jake says, "Talk to me, Leonard. You never talk to us."

I say, "Jake. You know I love you and all. But you're disturbing my thought pattern."

"That's just it," he says. "We never know what you're thinking. It's like you never let us in."

The soft rip of a piece of tape, then more blind smoothing under my fingers. I'm looking up, at the shadow.

"I'll make a deal with you. If you'll sit here with me

quietly, and not mess up my thoughts, I'll think them out loud for you."

"Seriously?" he says.

"Hush," I say. "Here's what I'm thinking.

"I'm thinking that if a boy drops into the world with-out a father, and without a name, it's almost like he didn't get here the same way everyone else did. Like the immaculate conception or something. Not to have a swelled head. I know Pearl was not a virgin. I don't kid myself. I know. It's just this feeling you get. This really dis-placed feeling.

"I'm thinking how when I went to kindergarten—oh, Jesus, now there's a whole other subject altogether. Anyway, don't distract me. I'm thinking how Mitch gave me his name. So for those three years I was Leonard Devereaux. But I knew I really wasn't. He wanted me to be but I wasn't.

"I'm wondering, what does that mean, to really wear somebody's name? If Mitch's name could be mine for real, if he had impregnated Pearl, would that change me? How would that change me? Would we be something different to each other?

"We would have lived together all this time. That's the part I can see. Not that you and Mona haven't been great."

Another soft rip of tape. I'm holding this long strip, feeling the stickiness under my fingers. I want to go on, but now I realize that it's not the same out loud with Jake here. It's not the same with somebody listening. Nobody ever listens to my thoughts, and now I realize I don't really want anyone to.

Besides, I want to think about things I can't tell him. Because he's part of my family, my adoptive people, and it's somehow important to them that I wear their name, like a new coat someone gives you because the old one was getting threadbare.

I was thinking about how sometimes I want to go back to using the name Devereaux, but I can't say that out loud. I know it would hurt Jake's feelings.

Also how sometimes I understand these kids who go off looking for their birth parents, because they don't really know who they are. And how other times I think that feeling, that disconnectedness of not knowing who I am, is on my side. It keeps me from getting too earthbound. From thinking this is some kind of final resting place, like home. But I can't feel all that in front of Jake.

"Tomorrow we'll take it out and inspect it in the light," I say. "Mount the harness."

I can feel him building himself up, to say something big. One of those critical human communications that seem so popular with everybody except maybe me, Leonard Nobody.

"We can't let you do this, Leonard."

"Okay. Fine. I understand."

I knew this would happen. I've already made up my mind not to fight it. It never helps to fight. You have to make like a piece of cheesecloth. Let 'em sweep right through you. No damage.

"What did you say?" he asks.

"You're right. I shouldn't do it. I'll call it off."

I hate like hell to lie to him, but it's kinder. I've already lied through my teeth to Mitch. I hated to do it. It goes against the grain. But it will be important for them in the long run. This way, if something goes wrong, they can say they didn't know.

And, anyway, this is something I need to do alone.

I'd like to think Jake believes me. But I think we both know that was way too easy.

After he leaves, I think about the time Mitch asked me why I was such a happy little guy. I was five years old. Pearl had been gone a few weeks. I thought really hard for an answer even though I think he'd gone about his business without expecting one.

Then I said, "I think it's because my mother loves me so much."

He gave me this look of utter pity, like I was the bravest kid in the world. He missed the point completely, you know? But he's my friend, anyway. There are just some things he doesn't understand.

### MITCH, *age 37*: leonard won't unpack

Monday morning, like clockwork, I arrive at my office and there's Mona, waiting to talk to me.

Here's the thing about Leonard: Leonard being Leonard, never any more or any less, every time I see Mona waiting for me I get this pitch inside my stomach, thinking what I might hear. If I were a parent for real, it would be the cops on my doorstep in the night. But much as I love that boy, much as I feel I have the right to call myself his parent, and much as he may see me as his true parent, Leonard could die and the police would never bother to come knocking. Likely I would hear it from Mona.

We make that initial eye contact, and I can tell it's not quite that bad. Not this time. And I breathe. And then I sigh. I haven't even hit my office door yet and already I've been fatally distracted.

"You gotta talk to him, Mitch," Mona says. "It's getting

worse. It's getting crazier. All the time. I'm so scared I'm going to lose him."

Me too, actually. But she's clearly come to me for comforting. And that would hardly qualify. "You want me to try to talk him out of the glider."

"Mostly. Yeah. But there's been some other stuff, too. And I just don't feel like we're getting through to him. Not like *you* always did. You could always get through to him."

To be polite, we both briefly pretend that wasn't a hard thing for her to admit.

I've noticed, too, lately, that Leonard has been dancing weirdly close to the edge of danger. Real, physical danger. He makes it sound like some kind of spiritual quest. But he is a human being, Leonard. Somewhere deep down he has the same makeup, the same basic urges as all of us. He just has this thing about transcendence. Doesn't want too many earthbound connections.

This makes me edgy because I get the sense that this is just a stopover for him, that he has no real plans for staying. Like if a guest came to my house and refused to unpack his suitcases. I might tease him about it. I might say, hey, loosen up and stay awhile. But the statement of intent would be pretty damn clear. That's Leonard's approach to life itself. He refuses to unpack.

"Is this about Pearl?" I say.

"Everything is about Pearl. You know what he thinks, don't you? I mean, he tells you, right? That he thinks Pearl is still with him?"

45

"He's learned not to talk about it around me," I say. "Because he knows he can't make the sale."

"When Pearl died—"

"*If* Pearl died," I say, more vehemently than necessary. Noticing how much vehemence I have gathered on this sore subject over the years. "*If* she died. No one knows for sure that she died. No body ever turned up. Leonard just decided she died. If you ask me, Pearl dropped him on my doorstep and took a powder. Can't you understand how important it is to him? Not to believe that?"

Mona decides to sidestep this entirely. She says, "He's getting pretty reckless, Mitch. He's so damn set on proving this theory about Pearl. But you see the danger, right? Because until he's dead, he won't know. I feel almost like he's trying to get closer and closer to that line. Talk to him, Mitch. Would you? He doesn't listen to me."

He doesn't listen to me, either, but I don't say so. "What do you mean, proving the theory?"

"Well, you know."

"If I knew I wouldn't ask."

"It's like he thinks this whole thing about dying . . . this thing everybody says about going into the light? Well, he thinks it's true enough, only he has this theory that it's . . . sort of . . . optional."

"Optional?" I say. It sounds stupid. I can't stop it from sounding stupid.

"Optional," she says. She has deep circles under her

already dark eyes. "He thinks if you don't want to go, you just don't. You stay. *With* somebody. Like he thinks Pearl did with him."

I want to ask what she believes, but then I decide it doesn't really matter. "Forever love," I say. Because that is something Leonard and I do talk about. He's been trying to teach me about forever love since he was five years old. I'm a slow learner, and he's patient.

Her face lights up at having finally found a common ground in this conversation. Something that we both understand that we both understand. My stomach lurches around almost painfully at the idea that Leonard is so hot to try this out.

"Okay," I say, steeling myself to say things that need saying. "Okay. Let's say, God forbid, the absolute worst happens. Worst-case scenario." I can't let myself spell it out any clearer than that. "Who is Leonard planning on hanging around to love?"

Mona's eyes go wide. Like she can't believe I wouldn't know. And I guess it embarrasses her to have to be the one to tell me. And also, it hurts her, because she wants it to be her but it's not.

She looks away again. "Well, you. Of course." Then, while I'm trying to swallow this meteorite of information, to dislodge it from its sticking place in my throat, she says, "Talk to him, Mitch."

And in a sudden fit of hopeless idiocy I agree that I will.

★ ★ ★

Leonard lives with his adoptive parents, Jake and Mona, these people he swears can never replace me. They have lots of kids, all adopted. Eleven, at last count. Many have special needs, so Leonard's vision problems, his asthma, just didn't strike them as a deterrent. Not like I was hoping it would. I was hoping nobody would take Leonard, and I'd get to keep him. But this do-gooder family had to crop up. Leonard and I have come to a fairly good understanding with it over the last decade. We pretend he belongs to them, and they let me visit. We know the truth, and where to keep it, and when to let it see the light. We belong to each other. In that instance, at least, Pearl showed a certain wisdom.

Leonard is in the family garage, just where Mona said he'd be. Working on his hang glider. Mona told me all about the glider, and about the tattoo.

He got the plans for the glider off the Internet. Then Jake hooked into some chat rooms, trying to find out what everybody thought of these home-built glider things. According to Jake's research, they're a big mistake. But here's Leonard in the family garage building one out of aluminum tubing, nuts and bolts, nylon mesh straps, and laminated polypropylene fabric.

Jake tried to find someone who had done the same thing successfully but was told they are all dead now. He was also told that if you are going to jump to your death, there's no need to build a hang glider to take along. He hopes these are "in" jokes for chat rooms but suspects that even "in" jokes get their start in the truth.

Leonard's faced away from me, looking so small and slight. Looking so bald, so monklike with his shaved head. I can see part of the tattoo. The top of the vertical beam of the cross. It rises just slightly up out of his collar. It's so detailed, right down to the rough wood grain. I have a lot of ambivalence about the tattoo, but right at the moment I am dying to see it all.

He's wearing his usual uniform: jeans and a plain white T-shirt. It offsets the color of his skin, which is somewhat magical in itself. Leonard is the color of coffee just exactly the way I drink it, with a generous splash of half-and-half. I can see the lump of his inhaler in his back jeans pocket. A beam of light sweeps down through the skylight in the roof and makes him look like the chosen one, which I often suspect he just might be. In that deep place where I believe almost nothing, I am tempted to believe that—a light, irritating tickle of belief. And the same beam of sun illuminates the weird silver skeleton of his craft-in-progress, nearly the length of the garage, and makes it look blessed.

I have to remind myself that I vehemently disapprove. This is the problem every time I see Leonard. I go in as a guidance counselor, come out as his personal cheerleader. Everything he does seems so right in person, and in proximity.

I just want to be left alone a moment to observe, but Moon Pie gives me away. Leonard's strange dog. A big wire-haired monster of a mutt, brown and featureless, slightly reminiscent of an Irish wolfhound but nothing quite so blue-blooded in the end. He thumps his tail, and I am made, busted. Leonard turns around.

"Mitch," he says. He always says my name like it's exactly the name he has been waiting to say.

"Leonard," I say and walk across his family's garage like I am walking in a dream. Clap one hand down firmly onto his shoulder.

"Mona sent you," he says. "Didn't she?"

"She means well."

"Duh," Leonard says. "That rather goes without saying."

Moon Pie's wet nose leaves a cold smear on the back of my hand. "Well, just to take her side for a minute, what the hell are you thinking, Leonard?"

He drops his head back into the light. Closes his eyes. As far as Leonard is concerned, I've asked a serious question. I'm not sure he even understands the concept of the rhetorical. He is working hard on giving me the serious answer my serious question so richly and obviously deserves.

"Well," he says, eyes still pressed closed in private prayer, "I'm thinking about Pearl. And I was thinking about you, just now. Right before you got here. And my eyes. I was thinking next time I see Mitch, I have to thank him again. For my eyes."

"You don't have to thank me for that anymore."

"Why not? I use my eyes every day. What else did Mona tell you?"

"Well, about the tattoo."

"They're almost never fatal."

"That's not entirely true. Are you sure this place uses sterile needles?"

"Positive. Want to see?"

And of course the crazy thing is, I do. I've had Mona describe it to me at great length.

One of his many little adoptive sisters runs in. A scrappy, scarred ten- or eleven-year-old who worships Leonard, as they all do. Everybody who needs love runs to Leonard, who seems to shepherd an inexhaustible supply.

"Hi, Leonard," she says. Eager and pleased. "Hi, Mitch." More reserved. "Can I help?"

"Nope, sorry. Gotta scram, little twerp. I'm about to show Mitch my tattoo."

"I wanna see it," she whines, already aching with the unfairness of being excluded from this exhilarating adult event.

"When you're eighteen," he says. "Otherwise I'll be corrupting you. You'll go out and get a tattoo and who will everybody blame? Me, that's who."

"Awww," she says, milking it a bit more.

Leonard tilts his head down. Gives her a look. "Fifteen minutes, I'll take you down the block for an ice cream. If you scram. And take Moon Pie with you."

Properly bought off, she runs out, holding the great shaggy beast's collar, slamming the small side garage door behind her.

Leonard pulls off his T-shirt. He has not one hair on his narrow little chest. I have this horror that some of his theatrics might get him thrown in jail. It literally makes me sweat to think how he'd fare in there. Lithe, smooth, hairless. Slight. Innocent inside and out.

He turns his back to me.

The tattoo is bigger than I realized. It starts just above the spot where the collar of his T-shirt lies and continues down the middle of his back. The horizontal beam extends across his shoulder blades and just beyond his shoulder on each side. So he has to stand with his arms out to show it off just right.

The wood-grain detail is so frighteningly realistic.

With him standing faced away like this, it almost reminds me of performance art. Which is something like my opinion of the kid anyway. Performance art.

I have to remind myself that I am somehow supposed to disapprove of this.

I am here not to admire the boy but to convince him, once and for good, that his dead mother is not here on earth with him. That his dead mother is, in fact, probably not even dead. That it's suicide to play these games, teasing at the edges of death as if he needed the practice. That if he loves me, he should love me right here, just like this, alive. And, also, I think I'm supposed to tell him the tattoo is foolish. I just can't remember why or on what grounds.

"Leonard. You don't . . . like . . . think you're . . . Jesus or anything. Do you?"

"You know me better than that," he says, still holding the pose. "So what do you think?"

"Well, it's beautiful. Really, it is. I'm just thinking . . . I'm just wondering if you'll still be glad to have it when you're . . . You know. Thirty."

He laughs. Turns around and takes the three or four steps across the garage concrete to me. Under the skeleton of his big dinosaur-bird craft. Still laughing. He touches my face as if I were his child, his silly paranoid child in need of comforting.

"Oh, Mitch," he says. I am so foolish. I can hear it in his voice. "Mitch. I'm not going to live to be thirty."

PEARL, *age* 17: **safe**

We got off the bus and there it was. The ocean. I had never seen such a thing before. My sweet little Leonard guy hadn't neither.

This was the day my boy turned four.

A birthday is a very big thing. It should be big from the minute you wake up. It should be such a big thing—all day long—that you fall down into sleep that night all worn out from so much bigness. You get a present with paper on it, you can open that in just a minute. And then, depending on what's inside, a birthday can sort of lose its shine. And then what do you got? No birthday. No big thing. So what I wanted for my sweet little boy was a birthday that would be big and last all day long.

Nobody should be able to mess with that, or make it not safe.

I had never seen the pier at Santa Monica but Rosalita had told me all about it. She said it's a big amusement place, and then it's a beach, all at the same time. She said it has a merry-go-round, and bumper cars, and an arcade where you can play Skee-Ball and win stuffed animals. Leonard didn't have no stuffed animals, so this was good. She said you can eat corn dogs and Sno-Kones and hot pretzels, and if you look between the boards of the pier you will see the ocean. Way down there under your feet. She said when it gets dark they turn on these big lights that shine out over the water, and they light up the white foamy parts of the waves coming in.

I never seen a wave coming in and Leonard neither, so that is a big thing.

I saved a long time for this. I cleaned a lot of houses to make this day be. You better believe that. Nobody should fuck with a thing like that.

Leonard took off his shoes and ran down onto the part of the sand where it's all wet and shiny, waiting for another wave to come in. When it did, it splashed up onto his shorts and curled all around his little skinny legs and he screamed. But it was good screaming.

"Pick me up, Mama," he said.

And I did, but I also wanted to know why.

"So I can see where it ends."

But even sitting up on my shoulders he still could not see the end of it.

See, that is a big thing.

★ ★ ★

We were on the sand with no towel but I don't think it mattered. Leonard didn't really have a thing to swim in, but he was in his boxer shorts and that worked out okay.

"You're going to get burned," I said.

"No, I'm okay," he said.

I was thinking we could go under the pier for shade but he liked it in the sun.

There is something nice about how your skin feels when the sun dries that salty water right onto you. It smells and feels like the beach.

Three guys walked by and one of them was drinking a beer and he winked at me, and I gave him a bad look for that.

He called me a filthy name.

I won't repeat it, but it's not the kind of thing you call somebody in front of her little boy. I will just say that and no more.

"I got my kid here," I said.

Because if I had said what I wanted to say, well, that's not something you say in front of your little boy, either. I was thinking if he did one more thing to make our big day less than perfect I might feel like I wanted to kill him. I'm not saying that I would have. Just that I was starting to think things like that.

The guy just stood there looking for a minute. He was not real steady on his feet in that sand. A big guy. One of his friends had walked on without him. The other one who stayed was a red-haired guy, not so big.

"Come on," the red-haired guy said and pulled the big drunk guy's arm. "Forget it," he said.

I think that's exactly what happened. I think the big drunk guy was so drunk he forgot what he was going to say, and so they walked away.

I was thinking how to remember this day so that part never happened.

Leonard had his mouth open, watching them walk away down the beach.

After a while it got to be three or four or five o'clock and we were pretty burned and the sun was way over to one side. It was getting nice and cool.

We went up onto the pier and Rosalita was right. You can look down between the cracks and that's the ocean. Down there. It makes you a little dizzy. It gives you this funny feeling inside.

We ate corn dogs and drank orange soda and then we had frozen Snickers bars for dessert. Leonard wanted to go on the bumper cars but I thought maybe not right after we ate. Maybe after a little while.

We walked around in the arcade and there were video games and driving games and Skee-Ball and on one wall was all the stuff you could win. I could see Leonard's face light up looking at all those stuffed tigers and giraffes and elephants and dolphins and horses and rabbits and pigs and bears.

I counted what money I had left, but it wasn't looking good for winning one. I would have to get every single ball in for fifty points and even then I wasn't sure it would be enough.

"Let's go ride the bumper cars," I said.

The guy in charge didn't want to let us on because Leonard wasn't big enough.

I said he could ride in a car with me, but he was not supposed to let people do that. But I would not get out of the way.

There was a line behind me and I wouldn't move out of it, and the guy behind us said, just let them go. He was mad at having to wait. So we got to go.

I rode with Leonard sitting between my knees. He was looking up at the ceiling. I think he was liking that electricity sound and those sparks from where the long poles on the backs of the cars touch the ceiling. Or not liking it, I don't know. Maybe a little bit of both.

But the drunk guy from the beach, he was on that ride, too, and he kept bumping us head-on. You are not supposed to bump head-on. It's against the rules. He was doing it just to be mean. And the guy in charge was not stopping the ride, either, to tell him. Maybe he was mad at me for getting on in the first place. I don't know.

I steered up beside the stupid drunk guy and I grabbed him by part of his sleeve. He was so drunk he didn't even think to knock me off him again. Not right away.

"Leave us the hell alone," I said. I sounded like I would hurt him if he didn't. I would have been scared of me, if I had been someone else hearing me say that.

Then we both crashed into a fat kid's car and the ride was over. I figured that would be the end of that.

We played Skee-Ball as long as we could. I mean, as long as the money was there to play with. It didn't go so good. In fact, it didn't go as good as I thought it would, and I'd never had what you might call high hopes.

Trouble was, my little sweet birthday guy wanted to play, too. How could I say no? It was his birthday, and he had never played Skee-Ball before.

But I wanted to win him a stuffed animal so bad. But what could I say to him? I had to let him try.

The first time he rolled the little ball, it didn't even go all the way up. After a few tries he rolled it real hard but never down the middle. Not for any points.

And I'd never played before, either. So I didn't get any points at first, and then after a while I'd get maybe a ten.

We were getting low on money. We had to save enough

for the merry-go-round and the bus back home. And we still only had one of those little tickets you get for playing good Skee-Ball. You can't get any prizes for one ticket. Not even the little stupid ones.

The drunk guy was playing way down on the other end of that arcade, and his red-headed friend was playing right next to him. Where the other guy went I didn't know. But they were good, and it pissed me off. I could see long strings of tickets hanging out of their Skee-Ball machines. At least they were leaving me alone.

But then the big drunk guy took out a cigarette. Only I don't think you could smoke in there. You have to step outside.

On his way out he walked right behind me. And he touched me. I swear to God that stupid asshole touched me.

Put his hand right on my ass.

I just completely went off.

I spun around and went at him and I was slapping him in the face and I think I kicked him once or twice. He fell backwards into a pinball machine and almost knocked it over. I was yelling about it being my boy's birthday, and how dare he go messing everything up like that?

He had this look in his eyes like he was going to come after me, but he never got to. Because his red-haired friend was there by that time, and also a guy who works in the arcade giving out change. And they held on to him and wouldn't let him come do whatever he was wanting to do back to me.

The red-headed guy said, "Stop it, Don. Just stop it. She's got a kid, okay?"

I turned around, and there was my little birthday guy, looking really scared. Why can't people just leave you alone?

The man who worked in the arcade told the drunk guy to get out and not come back.

He left mad, walked off down the stairs to the beach, and I'm happy to say we didn't see none of him after that.

The red-headed guy went back to the Skee-Ball machines and collected up all those tickets. There were two big long strings. He came up to us again. I knew he was not the bad one, but I wanted us left alone all the same.

"Sorry about my friend," he said.

I was looking at those long strings of tickets. It didn't seem fair. My boy deserved them a lot more. Why should a good thing like that happen to people who aren't even good people?

"You need different friends," I said.

"Don's not a bad guy. He just had a few too many."

He had that freckled skin that people with red hair have. I bet he couldn't spend too much time in the sun. He was older than me, but not old. Maybe twenty.

"Let me tell you about your friend," I said. "You stand too close to him, some of that stink might start to come off on you."

And I took my boy's hand and we walked away.

We were going riding on the merry-go-round.

Leonard got to pick out the horse. He picked one that was a silvery color, with a blowing mane. Its neck was all arched back.

We rode on that one horse together, and it was one of the ones that go up and down.

I closed my eyes and I was pretending it was a real horse, and that my boy Leonard and me were riding up and down hills with the ocean right down the hill from us. Which I could see really good with my eyes closed. I could smell the real ocean, which made it easy to pretend.

Leonard was kicking the horse's sides and telling him, "Go faster."

There was music.

When I opened my eyes that guy with the red hair and freckles was there watching, and he had a stuffed giraffe. He had traded in all his tickets for that nice stuffed toy, I guess. It didn't seem like the type of thing a guy would pick.

When the ride stopped we got off and he came up to us and tried to give the giraffe to Leonard. "For the birthday boy," he said.

First I wondered how he knew that, about Leonard's birthday, but then I remembered that I'd been yelling about it a lot.

I knew Leonard really wanted that giraffe, but half of those tickets were from that drunk asshole.

"We don't need nothing from you," I said.

And I turned my back on him once and for all.

The only money we had left was for the bus home. But then we would go home with nothing for Leonard to keep.

I turned back around, and the guy with the giraffe was gone.

There was a picture booth on one side of the merry-go-round building. The kind where you put in money and sit inside and pull the curtain. And it takes pictures of you and spits them out.

I felt kind of sick because I didn't know that before I spent all our money. We could have played a couple less Skee-Ball games and got our pictures took. That would be so perfect because it was us. And he would always have that, to remember the bigness of today.

I went over to that machine and put in the rest of our money. Maybe I should not have. Because now how would we get home? But I thought I would work that out somehow. I thought this mattered more.

We went inside and pulled the curtain behind us. There was a mirror. Leonard liked seeing us in a mirror. It made him smile. His front teeth were still gone. His glasses looked so big and thick. I wished he could have better ones. The lighter kind.

His hair was messy but it was okay. It looked sort of cute.

"Look at the mirror and smile," I said.

"And then what?"

"You'll see."

There was a big flash in our eyes and we both jumped.

Then I leaned my cheek down on top of his head. I did not want the camera to see in my eyes, because I was thinking how we'd get home. It flashed again and I kissed him on the side of his head because he is my boy. I knew we should get a picture of how much I love my boy.

Then there was one more, so I smiled at the camera and tried not to look scared.

Why can't people just be safe?

Especially when they're trying hard to do the best things they can.

We were walking on the pier and Leonard was looking down but it was too dark now. You couldn't see nothing between the boards.

Leonard was carrying that strip of pictures in his hand. Every now and then he would squint to see them again.

I was thinking maybe we would spend the night under the boardwalk and hitchhike home in the morning. I don't like to hitchhike at night. It isn't very safe.

I asked Leonard what he thought of that.

"What would it be like?" he wanted to know.

"Well," I said. "It would be an adventure."

"What's a venture like?"

"It might be cold," I said. "But it might be fun and exciting."

We went down the stairs and under the pier.

The night was cool now but a nice cool, and it was weird and nice to hear the ocean without seeing it. It was dark enough that you could only just barely see the white parts of the waves but you knew they were there from the sound. The sand was cold between our toes, and I was thinking it might not be a half bad adventure.

But we did not stay long, on account of there were people having sex down there. I took my boy by the hand and we walked away again.

"Those people looked like they were fighting," Leonard said.

"Well they weren't."

"Were they having a venture?"

"Maybe," I said. "I don't know."

This is when I decided once and for all that we had to go live some other place. Something about the drunk asshole and the people doing it under the pier. And that other thing. That older, worse thing. There had to be another place to live. Someplace that would be better for me and my sweet boy.

Where, I wasn't sure. But it should have an ocean. And it should be safe.

I said to Leonard, "Pretty soon we're going to move."

We were walking back toward the street, which is probably why he said what he did.

"We're moving now," he said.

"No, I mean to a whole new city."

"What one?"

"I don't know," I said. "A small one. With an ocean."

"Like Sanna Momica?"

"No. Much smaller. And safer."

"When?"

"I don't know. Soon."

We walked under the big arch sign and across the Pacific Coast Highway. I was thinking maybe I could pan-handle money for the bus. But for a while we just walked.

We were walking along Santa Monica Boulevard when the red-haired guy pulled up beside us. He had the window of his car down on our side. The giraffe was on the front seat with him. I could see the top of its head sticking up.

"You need a ride?" he asked.

I knew he would not hurt us, but I didn't want nothing from him. All the same. His car was one of those old ones. The kind a guy will buy to fix up. The kind a guy will cherry out and be real proud of. But his wasn't cherried out yet. Just real old.

"We don't need nothing from you," I said.

I looked down at Leonard and he still had those pictures in his hand, but he wasn't looking at them. I'm pretty sure he was looking at the giraffe. It made me feel bad.

"So you got a way to get home?"

We just stopped walking. I was feeling tired and sad. I wanted to be home. I wanted Leonard to have that giraffe. I wanted to live in a small place and be safe.

"We live far," I said. "Real far. All the way in Silver Lake." And we were lucky to live there. We had moved way up.

"I'll drive you. If you want."

We got into the backseat of his car.

He got on the freeway without talking.

His window was open, with his bare arm sitting on the edge of it. I felt the wind coming in. It blew my hair around. I watched the palm trees go by in the dark. I watched the shiny orange reflectors on the freeway flash by.

Leonard watched the head of the giraffe where it stuck up over the seat.

After a time the guy took a cigarette out of a pack and reached the pack back over the seat at me.

"Smoke?"

"No," I said. "I never would. It's a filthy habit if you ask me."

Instead of lighting his own cigarette he put it back in the pack.

"Real sorry about my friend," he said. Like he hadn't ever said that before.

"Get new friends," I said.

And we rode without talking nearly all the way to Silver Lake.

I had him drop us about three blocks from home.

"Why are we getting out here?" Leonard said.

And the guy said, "Because your mom doesn't want me to know where you live." We sat without talking for a minute. I did not get out because of that giraffe. I wanted him to offer it again so I could say yes this time. "Which is okay," he said.

Then I remembered that he was the guy who pulled the asshole away from me and told him I had a kid and to stop it. I was thinking I hadn't been very nice to him.

"Where would you move to," I said, "if you wanted to be safe?"

"Safe from what?" he asked.

"I don't know. This city, I guess. Everything."

"Oh. You mean like Don."

"Yeah. Like Don." And some others things I was not about to tell him.

We were sitting off to the side of Silver Lake Boulevard at a red curb where you are not supposed to park. Leonard was looking at the giraffe.

"No place is really guaranteed safe," he said.

"Some might be better."

"Maybe a small town."

"Has to have an ocean," I said.

"Well, maybe up the coast a ways. Santa Barbara is still pretty safe. There's a little town called Lompoc that's near a military base. And if you want really small you could try Morro Bay. That's probably a pretty safe place to live."

I was trying to learn those names in my head.

"Why can't people just leave me alone?" I said.

I looked up, and his eyes were watching me in the rearview mirror. "Maybe because you're nice-looking," he said. Then his eyes slipped away again.

"That's no good excuse," I said.

"No," he said. "I suppose not."

We sat quiet one more minute, and then he said, "I got no use for this at my house." He held the giraffe up by its neck. "I just got it for the kid. You sure he can't have it? He's been looking at it."

"Say thank you to the man for the present, Leonard."

"Thank you, mister," Leonard said. And he took the stuffed giraffe into the backseat with us.

For a minute I felt bad. Because what about what I gave Leonard? That didn't seem so important anymore.

Only then Leonard said to the guy, "Look what else I got." And he showed him the pictures we took of us in the merry-go-round house.

I felt better then.

"Hey, nice," the guy said. "You and your mom. That's a nice thing to have to remember today."

"Yuh," Leonard said. "I know. You want one?"

"Me?" the guy asked. Kind of surprised sounding.

Leonard is a very generous boy. People aren't always ready for how generous he can be.

"Yuh. I got four. See? We'd have to have a way to cut one, though."

"No," the guy said. "I think you should keep all four, because it's your birthday."

" 'Kay," Leonard said. "Bye."

"You're a lucky boy. To have a mom who takes such good care of you."

"Yuh," Leonard said. "I know."

We got out and walked the rest of the way home.

The night felt good on my skin.

I looked around once and the guy was watching us go. He had lit a cigarette and was smoking and watching us walk home.

But then we turned a corner and he didn't try to follow. He let home be a secret thing from him.

He let us be safe.

Leonard slept with the pictures on his pillow. He slept all wrapped around the giraffe. In the morning I asked if I should put the pictures somewhere safe.

"Where?" he wanted to know.

"I don't know. Somewhere they can't get hurt or lost."

"Can I still see them whenever I want?"

"Anytime you want."

" 'Kay, then," he said. "I think so."

★ ★ ★

For days I looked into every car I walked by.

Most cars don't have the keys left in, but one always will. If you look into enough cars, for enough days, one will always have the keys left in.

Then you can go wherever you need to go.

On our way up the coast it was night, and Leonard looked over at the moon and said it was racing us. He wanted to know who I thought would win. I told him I thought it would come out a tie.

Then he slept the whole rest of the way.

LEONARD, *age 5*: **dangling dog**

When I got dropped at Mitch's house, he was watching the six o'clock news. After Pearl left I sat down and we watched together.

It had been raining for a long time. Days.

On the news they were showing this guy being helicoptered out of the big concrete river thing. He'd been walking his dog in there, and then the water came up and the save-you team had to go in and get him. And get the dog. Saver-guy put on a harness and they lowered him on this rope, and he held on to the guy and the guy held on to his dog and then they just flew on out of there.

I put my hands over my eyes. Well, over my glasses. I cupped my hands over my glasses so I couldn't see, but so I wouldn't have to take them off and clean them after. You learn these things.

"What?" Mitch said.

"I can't look."

"You afraid he's going to drop that dog?"

"Don't tell me," I said. Last I'd seen, the dog was just kind of dangling there. Swinging. And the guy had him under the arms. A big dog, like a German shepherd but maybe some other things, too. I'm sure the guy was holding on fierce tight, but it looked iffy. "Only tell me if it turns out okay."

A few seconds went by and then Mitch said, "It's okay."

I took my hands down off my glasses.

They were already on to another story.

"What was wrong with your mom?" he said.

"I dunno," I said. "I thought everything was fine."

Later that night he had put me to bed on his couch downstairs. But he was still watching TV. It was this cop show.

The cops were all the good guys.

He was sitting next to me on the couch and I think he thought I was asleep. I could hear Pebbles and Zonker making little happy noises in the corner.

I guess I must have started to sing. But I wasn't really thinking about the fact that I was singing. I was just doing it.

"What's that?" Mitch said.

"What's what?"

"Why aren't you asleep? What's that thing you're singing?"

It was the song Pearl and I used to sing at bedtime.

"It's nothing," I said.

"Why aren't you asleep?"

"I dunno," I said. "Just can't."

I sat up and put my glasses on and we watched the rest of that cop show together. You could tell exactly who the bad guys were, and they got theirs in the end.

Then the eleven o'clock news came on, and they showed the guy with the dog again, hanging from the helicopter.

I put my hands over my glasses again.

"Leonard," Mitch said. "Buddy. If he didn't drop that sucker on the live footage, he's not going to drop him on the video replay."

"Yuh," I said. "I knew that."

I woke up late. I think I was having a dream about Pearl. But I couldn't hang on to it. It kept sliding away. It was like trying to grab a handful of water.

I sat up and couldn't find my glasses in the dark. I couldn't find my inhaler. I couldn't breathe and I couldn't see to find my glasses without my glasses. I'd never been at Mitch's house in the night before.

I knew Pearl was there with me, but I didn't really know what that meant yet. And besides, I needed my inhaler even worse.

PEARL, *age* 18: **it's something**

Two things I worked very hard at during those five years after Leonard came. One was talking better. The other was not getting arrested.

I figured, I more or less knew how to talk. I just didn't really practice. You know, what with spending so much time on the street with those people who don't know, or don't know how to use what they know. But I went to school almost eight years. I thought I could do it if I tried, and Leonard was my reason to try. A boy looks to his mother. Anyway this is what I believed.

As far as getting arrested, at first I was even scared to go see Rosalita in jail. But she paid cash for that apartment every month and the landlord did not know her name nor care. But I was that careful at first. Then after a while, since you never get arrested, you start thinking maybe you never will.

So for five years I practiced this good talking thing and did not get arrested. And then one day I did.

I was running an errand for Mrs. Morales, in her car. She has a very nice car, which I think is why I got pulled over. I didn't look nice enough to go behind the wheel. Anyway I pretty much knew how to drive from Rosalita and her car, which she let me use while she was in jail until it died. It was not nearly so nice. But I did not have no license. Any license, I mean.

They took me down to the station and took my pictures front and side and my fingerprints. This is bad, I thought. This is really really bad. But then they said, we are going to cite you out. I didn't know what that meant. Turns out it means I get this ticket. They said I had to come back for court and pay a fine. And when I went to court, they said, I would have to show ID, which I did not have on me that day. But I lied about my name. So I could not ever show any ID in that phony name. I thought real hard which was worse, a lie or the truth. I ended up with the lie, but I still don't know what was better. I don't know that it matters either way. It was all over as of that day.

I thought, I will take Leonard and we will go away. Only even farther this time. Maybe up to Oregon or Washington State, which they say is real nice. So long as we could be together I thought it didn't matter much where that was.

\* \* \*

On the day I had to go to court, I left Leonard at Doc's house. He stayed there a lot and he seemed to like it. I think they were all pretty nice with him. Except that one bird.

I took the bus.

I thought I'd be out of that town and on to Oregon before I had to go to court, and of course now I know I should've been. It's always easy to look back later and see what you should've known. Anyway I asked the judge for another thirty days to earn the money. It was true I needed more time, but the money I earned I was never planning to give to any judge. Me and Leonard we were going to buy a bus ticket and get the hell away. Judge asked about my ID and I told him my mother had it and she'd gone out of town and I did not know how to get in touch with her, but I'd bring it when I came back. I know how it is with them. Cops, judges, they are pretty much the same. If they want they can say that's not good enough. Or if they want they can shake their head and say I don't care, just go away. He shook his head and said I had thirty days to straighten it all out.

When I got back on the bus it was raining. There was this big dark American car. It was just sitting there. I don't even know why I noticed it, except when I got off the bus at my street it was there again. Or maybe it was another big dark American car. Don't get spooky,

I said to myself. Pearl, don't tell those stories to yourself.

I got Leonard back and we went home, and I put him to bed and sat there with him, stroking back his hair and singing and telling him how we would go live someplace new. What would it be like? he wanted to know. I didn't know myself, but he wanted to know, so I made stuff up for him. All of it was pretty and good, and I stroked back his hair and sang and told him about it until he went to sleep.

I didn't have to work the next day. Only for Mrs. Morales. But sometime around six in the afternoon we had to walk down to the drugstore to get her prescription filled. I thought Leonard could just come along. We stepped out of the house together. It was a pretty afternoon. The rain had stopped and the air smelled nice. Then a car pulled up behind us. It was a big dark American car. I looked over my shoulder. I didn't see who was driving the car but I saw the man in the shotgun seat. He had his window down, looking right at me. I knew him right away. I'd been waiting to see him. Every day I stepped out of the house, every house we'd lived in since that birthday when I was thirteen, I had looked up thinking he'd be there. And now he was.

I took Leonard hard by the arm. Usually I don't like to yank him around, but I was scared and upset. My stomach was all cold and strange, and I felt like maybe I had to pee and couldn't stop that if it happened. But it didn't come to that, thank God.

LOVE IN THE PRESENT TENSE

"Come on, Leonard," I said.

And he said, "Ouch. My arm."

I took him to the door at Doc's place and then inside, and as I did I looked back. The car pulled up and stopped in front of the house and I knew he was going to wait for me.

Doc looked at me. "Pearl," he said. "What happened? What's wrong?"

I had thought I was being so cool about things. I said, "I'm not really sure how long Leonard will have to stay this time. It's an emergency. Okay?"

Then I got down on my knees and grabbed hold of him and held him tight. Really really tight. "Ow," he said. "When are you coming back?"

I knew then that I was scaring him, so I let go and I walked away without looking back. I didn't want him to see my face.

The man with the lip was waiting for me. Watching for me to come back out the door. He could see me through the window the whole time, so he was just waiting. I thought maybe I should run, but my knees felt funny and I thought he would catch me anyway.

"Gonna get in the car on your own?" he said.

I thought about my dignity, and the promise I had made to myself, and I walked over to his car and got in.

★ ★ ★

We been driving a long time now. First I thought, he is taking me to jail. Now I don't think so. It's getting dark and we are driving south I think. Maybe he is going to take me to jail in L.A. But I don't really think so. I think then they would stay on the big road. The freeway. We are going way out in the middle of nowhere. It's dark out and we're going up high, like in the mountains, where I never been.

Nobody has said nothing so far.

Then the guy with the lip, he looks back at me. He has his arm over the seat and he turns around and gives me this look. His face is set hard like a mountain. I guess he needs it to be. He looks at me with so much hate.

Something funny happens when he looks at me. I can't probably explain it right, but it feels like I get outside me and I can still see all this, but not from inside where I always live. More like from a place over my shoulder.

The guy who is driving has blond hair and he is nice to look at. At least on some other day he might be. I look at the rearview mirror and see his eyes there. He doesn't hate me as much. He wants to, but he can't quite hate me as much and that's bothering him.

The lip man says, "Sooner or later you were gonna get arrested. Didn't I say that, Chet?" Chet I guess is the pretty blond man. "I went through every mug shot of every girl under twenty-one, everywhere in California, every week. It was only a matter of time."

I think, it takes an awful lot of hate to do that. That

must've been a lot of trouble. But the part of me over my shoulder says, no. Don't say that. Don't say nothing. It won't help. And also, dignity. It says, remember that.

I am sitting in the dirt. In the dark. But there is some moon, and some stars. It has been raining nearly five days, so this night is real clear. The ground is wet and soaks through my clothes. My hands are in cuffs behind my back so I won't run away.

Right now the blond man is sitting on a rock and the man with the lip is standing near me holding his gun. I can't see the lip in this light, but in another way that's all I can see. I just close my eyes and I see it.

"Christ, Benny," the blond pretty man says. Nobody has said nothing until now. He says, "She's just a kid. For Christ's sake."

The lip man says, "He wasn't your partner."

"Let's just take her in."

"And put his family through that? Put his wife and kids through knowing what happened with her? I don't think so. I think they deserve better. She's gonna get her story straight right here and now. Or she won't ever be going in." All that hate is still right there. But it feels to me like he's having to work harder now to make it stay.

I think they are trying to start by getting me really scared so I will do whatever they say. But I don't know what they will say. So I don't know if I'll do it.

Right now I'm not really thinking anything, being more over my shoulder and calm. Not normal calm, though. Too calm. Kind of scary calm. But I'm not thinking much. After a while I guess I start to sing. I don't even think about it while I'm doing it. I don't know I'm singing until the lip guy, he says, "What is that?"

Nobody has asked me any straight-out questions until now. I was thinking I would not have to talk. Now that he reminds me, it's the song I used to sing with Leonard at night before he went to sleep.

But Mr. Lip does not need to know this. This is between me and my boy.

"It ain't nothing," I say.

"Ain't nothing," he says, like an echo. He is making fun of me. "Don't you know how to talk?"

Yes I do but you made me forget again. I practiced hard but you scared me into a place where I forgot.

"It isn't anything," he says.

Yes, it is. It is everything.

Blond man looks like he wants to get this over with, whatever it is. I can see his face in the light from the moon. Not all that good, but I can. He is scared and not sure. He doesn't have nearly enough hate. He is reaching for more but it fails him. I can tell this. I can see.

"Jesus Christ, Benny," he says. "Let's just take her in already."

"And put his family through that? No fucking way. I

don't think so. Not when all they have is their memory of him. Not when so many good cops worked so hard to make sure they never had to know he died with his pants off. No, she's gonna get her story straight. And then we'll see whether or not we're going in."

I can tell by his voice that he's making it sound as bad as he can to scare me.

I'm looking up at a star. I can feel the cuffs behind me, and I try to rub my wrists where the cuffs are cutting in and hurting. But I really can't.

I'm not over my shoulder anymore. That's too bad. I thought that would keep up. This is a bad place for that to leave me. I feel the end of his gun, right in that little hollow at the back of my neck. Either the gun is shaking or I am shaking. I didn't know I was shaking but maybe I am.

"What have you got to say for yourself?" he says. His voice sounds different. He is scared and upset. I can hear this and feel this all, right now, and I feel sorry for him. "You tell me the truth, right now. Then we'll go over what you say in court."

"I'll tell the truth in court," I say.

Maybe he will hurt me for saying that. Or even kill me. But he already wants to put me in jail for all my life and that's worse. That puts me even farther from Leonard. Nobody keeps me from Leonard. And, also, nobody gets my dignity.

"Oh," he says. "Oh, you're a cold-blooded little skank, aren't you?"

Right now, yes, my blood feels very cold.

"Here's what I see," he says. "You came on to him, you lured him up to your place, laid him, shot him like a dog for his credit cards and the money in his wallet. Took advantage of a weakness in him. That's what I see. A wife and three little kids at home. Three little orphans."

I think, who are you telling all this to? There's nobody here but us. I think, that's wrong. You're not an orphan until both parents are dead. Leonard was not an orphan when his father got shot. I hope he won't be by the end of tonight. But I don't say that. I don't say anything.

"What about the guy who went down for this?" he says. He is sounding scareder now, talking in more of a hurry. "That Julius Banks. Was he the guy in charge? Did he force you to do this? If he did, you better tell me fast."

"Little Julius didn't have nothing to do with it," I say.

I wonder if he will go back now and let Little Julius out of jail. But he won't. Still, he knows and I know that this is more or less okay, because Little Julius did lots of stuff he should go to jail for but just did not get caught. Now he got caught for something he shouldn't go to jail for. It kind of works out in the long run.

"Well, whether you like it or not, you'll leave out what happened between you and Len when you go to court. His family is never to know. You lured him up there to rob him. That's all there was to that."

"I'll tell the truth in court," I say.

I'm not trying to make him mad. Not when he has the

gun and all. But I will never have my sweet little boy thinking his mother would kill somebody for some credit cards and money. It will never end like that.

"You can't say that to me," he says. He sounds like he is so mad he doesn't even know what to do with himself. Like he can hardly talk. "I got the gun." He pokes the gun harder into that little hollow of my neck. I guess to remind me who's got it. It hurts but I don't say ouch. "You'll do what I say. You got no choice." He sounds like he will turn inside out if he can't make me see that. If I won't agree. I think he forgot to make a plan for if I won't agree.

"I got a choice," I say. I choose not to let Leonard think I killed some guy on purpose for credit cards. No matter how upset it makes anybody. No matter what.

"You got to the count of three," he says. His voice sounds like he is crying. I didn't know big men cried. "I'm going to count to three."

"Benny?" The blond man is getting really scared. "Benny? You're still just trying to scare her, right?"

"I'm not letting her run this show. I'm not letting her hurt his family any more than they been hurt already. He wasn't your partner. You in or out? You tell me right now. Whose side are you on?"

"I got a kid nearly her age, Benny. Don't let that temper of yours make you do something you can't ever take back. Please, Benny."

Nobody says nothing for a long time. I'm sorry to hear the man with the gun has a temper.

"Go wait in the car why don't you?" Benny says.

"Benny—"

"Go wait in the car. I mean it. Stay out of this for a minute."

"Jesus," he says again. But he goes and waits in the car. I was hoping he wouldn't.

I look up at one of the stars. A big one hanging over that big slope. That star looks strange. A ray of its light seems to come out in my direction. That's how I know I am crying, too. The way the tears bend that light. Make it do something I don't think it otherwise would.

"One."

I think it's sweet and sad and maybe kind of strange, too, that we are crying, both of us, together, like this is something we can share. Like as far apart as two people can get, there is still something they can share.

I'm still pretty sure he isn't going to do it. That he's just so sure I'll give up and say what he wants when he gets to three. But I won't. And I think we might be getting close up to this line where he's so mad that even *he* doesn't know what he'll do when I don't. I can feel him come up to that line. I can hear it in his voice. And even in the silence. I can hear something important in the silence. As he comes up to that line. His temper is bigger than he is. It gets big and then he can't tell it what to do.

Then I think I should have told Doc all about Leonard's health stuff. How will anyone know about his eyes? Twice every year he is supposed to have screenings for his eyes, on account of this condition he has because of being borned too soon. There could be problems later on, and someone needs to know to check. Who will know this? I wonder. While I'm in jail. Or whatever.

"Two."

I think about that song we used to sing, me and Leonard, that little nonsense song, and I sing it again. But loud now, not under my breath. I really fill up my lungs now and sing it nearly loud enough for him to hear. Except I know it's really not loud enough for him to hear. I am only pretending that. But I bet the blond man in the car can hear me. I wonder if it makes him cry.

"Three."

The light from that star reaches out like it wants to touch me. And I know that in just a second I will be able to jump out and meet it halfway.

I hear the hammer click back on the gun.

The first thing I will do when I get out of here is head on back to my boy.

## MITCH, *age 25*: **breathe**

"It's raining again," she said. "Why is Leonard still here?"

She was standing in that narrow space between my bed and the window, trying to get her dress unzipped. I could smell the rain and her perfume, or so I thought. She seemed slightly disheveled, her hairstyle flattened by the moisture, which suited me just fine. The more disheveled the better. When fully dressed and made up, she seemed a little too . . . I can never find the word I'm searching for. Conservative? Feminine in that very traditional sense? Old?

Goddamn me. Bite my tongue.

The most exciting image I ever held and nursed was a moment I spent in the shower with her, the hot water rushing over our faces, running into our mouths when they came together or apart, her hair plastered onto her face, makeup down the drain. All that other crap I was just trying to find the words for, down the drain. I nursed that one for months, but it faded. In time they all do.

"I don't know," I said. "Some kind of emergency with Pearl."

She was taking off her panty hose standing up. She could do that without falling down or looking the least bit undignified. Good thing I was not born a woman. There are skills involved. I'm not sure I could handle them.

"What if she comes back now?"

"She won't come back in the middle of the night," I said.

"Why not?"

"All the lights are off. She'll come in the morning."

"I suppose."

She still hadn't managed to get her dress unzipped.

There's a skylight over the bed. And a streetlight on a hill above, so that even on nights with no moon I had a little glow of light to help me see her. We made love every possible way except with the lights on. That was out of the question for her.

The rain beaded up on the skylight and reflected onto her face and her dress as she took off her half-slip. "What if he wakes up?"

"Why should he wake up?"

"Kids wake up."

She had raised two to maturity, so who was I to argue? "Tell you what," I said. "As a concession to young minds, we'll do it under the covers."

She came over and sat on the edge of my bed—faced

away—offering me her zipper, though it took me a moment to get the hint. "That would be different," she said. "For us that would be almost kinky. You want to unzip me?" She held her hair aside.

Right. Of course. "I live to unzip you," I said.

I got up on my knees behind her and then sank down onto my haunches, so I was sitting on my heels. One knee on either side of her, close up against her back. I had to lean back a little to undo the zipper. Then I slipped the dress forward over her shoulders. Unhooked her bra. She leaned back and made a small, comfortable noise. My hands traced a path up her rib cage, finding her small breasts from underneath.

I was naked, for two reasons. Because I'd known to expect her. And because that's how I do bed, even alone. Well, three reasons. I'm not as adept as she is at peeling out of my clothes with grace.

"Those banquets are so intolerably boring," she said. "All I could think about was getting out of there and getting over here to you."

Then she attacked me. In a good way, I mean. She had a habit of sudden sexual aggression. She turned all the way around and threw me back down on the bed in one sudden motion. Which I would not have minded except that I ended up with one ankle pinned painfully underneath me, and the weight of my body being thrown back really twisted it hard. For a minute I was actually distracted by that pain.

"Ow?" she said. "Ow what?" I didn't know I had said that. But she was straddling me at this point, both of her small, graceful hands wrapped around a key body part. We were both willing to accept "ow" as a good thing.

That touch. The one I'd been waiting for, falling back on in my mind every 6.7 seconds for the past nine days. Hard to imagine there could be a downside to it. But there was. She hadn't taken off her ring, and I could feel it.

I know she always thought I made too much of that. But a guy has a right to feel the way he feels. I took hold of her left hand. Held it up between us. Removed it for her.

"Oh, that," she said.

"Yeah. That." I put it on the bedside table.

"Do *not* put it there," she said. By then I should have known better. "I'll forget it. Damn it, Mitchell, what if I get home and don't have it with me? What the hell am I supposed to say?"

I don't know. The truth?

I picked it up and dropped it into her purse, which was conveniently located on the floor, right where the night-stand met the bed.

She leaned over, peered off the edge of the bed into her purse like she was looking down a bottomless pit. "Great," she said. "Now it's in the Bermuda Triangle. It may never be seen again. Well, never mind. At least it goes home with me."

And with that she did something strangely un-Barb-like. She stretched her body the full length of mine and lay on top of me, up on her elbows just enough to look down at my face. She touched my cheek.

Every now and then some barrier would break away or break down, and she would reward me with a moment smacking of something like romance. And all I had to do was run a couple of thousand miles and swim an ocean or two to get it.

The rain-mottled light from above was good enough to allow me to see her mouth, which so defined her, and a trace of the laugh lines at the corners of her eyes. I loved them, but had long since given up saying so. Or trying to touch them. Though I wanted to, badly. I couldn't really see colors, though, so the impact from her eyes got lost. She has fabulous eyes, Barb. So dark blue they're almost navy. And hair moving from dark blond to gray in a natural, unimpeded progression.

This was all very important, you see, because it was part of a process by which I memorized these visuals, to hold me over until she next came back to see me.

She tucked her face against my neck, and I could feel the warmth of her breath between my neck and collar-bone. The moment continued.

"Don't go home tonight," I said. "Stay with me."

I'm a suicide bomber when it comes to love.

I could feel her sigh. Feel the air on my neck, and her

chest expand against mine. Her back rise and fall under my hands. I could feel my ankle throb.

"Oh, Mitchell," she said. "Why do you always want the one thing you know I can't give you?"

"Never mind. Forget I asked."

Amazingly, we both managed.

It was such an intense moment that the lines blurred between pain and pleasure, and I'd begun to think my ankle had become an erogenous zone. Every bit of friction seemed to radiate into that ache and radiate back as a desirable feeling.

I heard the scratchy breathing, but it never occurred to me that it didn't belong. The room was full of every kind of breathing, anyway. No sound could really surprise me.

Then I felt that little hand touch my shoulder, and I jumped. And Barb jumped. And we ended up side by side, on our backs, the sheet pulled up under our chins.

"Leonard," I said. "What are you doing up?" No answer. Just that catchy breathing. I wasn't putting two and two together right. I thought it was an emotional thing, like crying. "Leonard, you need to go back to bed. Come on. I'll take you back to bed. Well, in a minute. Give me a minute, I'll tuck you in."

"Mitchell," Barb said. "He can't breathe."

"Oh, my God." She was right of course. Everybody

knew these basic things except me. "Leonard, buddy. Where's your inhaler?"

He shrugged desperately, an apparent pantomime for "Help!"

I shot out of bed. Grabbed him up and threw him under my arm. I was uncomfortable with being naked around him (his mother thinks maybe I molest little boys), but I didn't feel like that was important now. Or, at least, I was not willing to prioritize that over his oxygen supply. I navigated the treacherous ladderlike steps from my loft to the downstairs, favoring my twisted ankle but still using it in a way I probably could not have without the adrenaline.

I put him down, turned on the light, and looked around. He was right. It was nowhere.

I panicked. Threw couch cushions around. Shook blankets. Threw magazines off the coffee table.

A minute later I felt Barb's hand on my back and I turned around. She was wearing my khaki shirt, which came down almost to her knees. She pointed to the bird-cage. Pebbles had the inhaler. Holding it in one monstrous talon, using her beak to try to separate the tan plastic from the shiny metal cartridge. The prize.

"Goddamn it, Pebbles," I said. I ran at her with such panic and intensity that she dropped the damn thing and backed into the corner of the cage. And Pebbles was afraid of nothing. I grabbed it up, but it was filthy. I couldn't give it to him in that condition.

"Shit," I said. "Shit, goddamn it, this has bird shit on it. He can't put this in his mouth. Shit." This from the man who said "language" in a conservative tone every time one of my employees swore in front of Leonard.

Barb grabbed it out of my hand. "Go sit with him," she said. "Talk to him." She gave me a little push.

I sat down on the couch with him. He'd been sitting with his arms wrapped around himself. Like he was holding himself until I could get there. I pulled him up onto my knees. He was wearing a T-shirt I'd given him to sleep in. A floor-length dress to him. But at least one of us wasn't naked. I took over for him, wrapping my arms around him and holding him tight. "We gotcha covered, buddy," I said. "We're just about to work this out."

I knew that if Pearl were here she'd say, "Okay. Leonard can't stay here anymore. I've decided it's not okay." She would have no patience with my poor skills in crisis.

Barb came back out of the kitchen, drying the now clean inhaler with a dish towel. She sat on the coffee table, her bare knees bumping up against mine. Held it up for Leonard to take.

"Know how to take it from here?" she asked him. She sounded calm; how did she do that?

Leonard nodded. Took the inhaler in both hands, held it facing himself. I could see the dents Pebbles had made in it with her beak. I could feel the jump of his tiny back as he gasped it in. I waited, but he still didn't seem to be breathing.

Barb must've read my mind. "It takes a minute," she said. She put her hand on my arm. Her left hand. I looked down at it. I could see a tan line where the ring had been. "Mitchell," she said, to pull my attention back. "Don't hold him so tightly."

"What?"

"You're holding too tight around his chest."

"Oh. Right."

"If you panic, he'll panic," she said. "Breathe." I thought she meant Leonard. I thought that was callous advice. If he could, he would. "Mitchell," she said. "Breathe."

I pulled a deep chestful of air. I hadn't noticed that I hadn't been breathing. I loosened my grip on Leonard's chest.

Barb turned her attention down to Leonard's little face. She held up one finger. "Grab hold of this," she said, and he did. "Pebbles took your inhaler. Bad Pebbles, huh?"

Leonard nodded. Tried to say something. Tried to say "Yuh," I think, but it came out sounding like a needle pulled across an old phonograph record.

"What kind of noise does Pebbles make, Leonard? Do you know?"

He nodded again. Didn't try to talk. But she had his undivided attention. His attempts at breathing had grown less gaspy, more shallow.

"Mooo. Is that what Pebbles says?"

A funny sound came out of him, and I felt his little body shake. I thought he was in some kind of pain or spasm. Then I realized he was giggling. "Nah," he said, and I could make the word out.

"Quack quack."

More giggling, deeper and happier this time. "Nah."

"What does she say, then?"

"Squawk!" His breathing had morphed into that of a runner at the finish line of a marathon. Normal but depleted. Taking in air, but with a serious debt to repay.

"Sounds right to me," she said, and she ruffled one hand through his hair.

I set my chin down on Leonard's shoulder and just watched her. How did she learn all this? What the hell would I have done if I'd been here alone?

She looked up and caught my eye. "Don't look at me like that," she said. "It makes me nervous."

In a rare display of acting in my own best interests, I didn't ask her to define "like that."

"Why don't you go put some pants on?" she said.

## LEONARD, *age 5*: **the first perfect moment**

Mitch carried me up to his loft, piggyback. He'd put on a pair of sweatpants but his back was still bare. I couldn't really wrap my legs around him because that big T-shirt came all the way down to my ankles. So I just sort of held on and dangled there. I was actually fine by then and he knew it. He just gave me the lift to be friendly and nice.

He lit a candle, because I was funny about him turning off the lights. Usually I wasn't all that scared of the dark. But I think I was still a little weird from waking up in a new place, and it had been dark, and I couldn't find my inhaler.

Mitch was lying in his bed with me. Barb came up and she was wearing a big long shirt that I think was Mitch's. She started picking up her clothes.

"Oh, no," Mitch said. "You're leaving? Don't leave." He

begged her to stay for just a few minutes. "We'll just talk," he said.

She pulled back the covers and got in beside Mitch. I had my hands clasped behind my head, looking up at the ceiling. Watching that candlelight dance around on the beams and plaster. I wiggled my head back and forth to play with the light, and I could feel the elastic strap of my glasses slip back and forth.

Out of the corner of my eye I saw that Barb had her hand on Mitch's chest. And Mitch had his hand on my chest. It was nice.

"Okay," Barb said. "What should we talk about?"

I looked straight at that candle flame and I knew everything was okay. It was like . . . Pearl.

It was my first perfect moment.

"Tell Barb about the dog," Mitch said.

"The one that gets walked down our street in the morning?"

"No. The one on the TV."

"Oh, yuh," I said. "You should have seen it, Bar. It was totally cool. This guy was walking his dog and the water got high and the dog was like dangling under this helicopter and I thought the guy was gonna drop him. Twice we saw it. I covered my eyes both times, just to be safe. I know I didn't really have to. It was just to be safe."

"Yeah, you can't be too careful," she said.

Then we were quiet for a long time. I closed my eyes. I was looking at the light from the candle through my eyelids, and even that was sort of still like Pearl. But then after a while I know Mitch thought I was asleep, because he took off my glasses and set them on the bedside table. It started to rain again, and I could hear it on the skylight over my head, and the rain was sort of like Pearl, too.

It was a really perfect moment.

LEONARD, *age 17:* **the first perfect moment**

Question: How many angels can dance in the flame of a lighted candle? Answer: Only one but that's enough.

Some things I remember bizarrely well about that night. Little scraps of seemingly unimportant moments that will never go away. They are permanently engraved, a part of me now. Lots of other whole segments are gone. But certain things I remember. Only, maybe I don't remember the actual events anymore. Maybe I just remember remembering.

Then again, whatever.

Here's all that matters: I looked straight at that candle flame and I knew Pearl was with me in that light. It was my first perfect moment.

Then, after they thought I was asleep, they started to talk quietly, and I knew they thought I was sleeping, and I let them think that. Not that I wanted to snoop so much.

I think I was at that age where it was hard for me to understand that the world kept going while I was sleeping. It was like cheating sleep—hearing what I'd missed every single night of my life.

Barb said, "Know what they call that guy dangling from the cable?"

Mitch said, "What who calls him?"

"Rescue personnel, dispatchers, police. It's kind of an inside language."

"I give up," Mitch said. "What do they call him?"

"Either a tea bag or a dope on a rope. Depending on how charitable they're feeling."

"Why is he a dope? Because he wasn't supposed to be walking his dog in a flood basin?"

"We're talking two different things," she said. "You're talking about the rescuee. I'm talking about the rescuer."

"Now I'm really confused," Mitch said. "Why is *he* a dope?"

"Because he's out there risking his life for some idiot who should never have been walking his dog in a flood basin to begin with. I'm telling you, Mitchell. Most people who need rescuing need it because they were doing something any fool should know better than to do in the first place. The older you get the more you see that. They're going to bill that guy for his own rescue. You watch."

"I really feel sorry for the dog," Mitch said. "He's just along for the ride and it's so completely out of his control."

They didn't talk for a minute and then Barb said, "It doesn't pay to be the dog, Mitchell."

I've thought a lot about what she meant by that, both then and since. It could be taken at face value, but that's not the way she said it. It didn't feel like a toss-off comment. It sounded like she was trying to teach him something, but I'm not sure what, because if you're the dog you just are, and nothing you learn will ever change that.

Then after a while I heard some sounds that I think might have been a kiss, but I didn't open my eyes. But I heard little soft breaths, and that wet noise like mouths coming together and then apart again.

"Oh, God," Mitch said, and he was whispering. "Don't get me started."

I didn't know at the time what he meant by that but I could feel his hunger. It felt needy and straining, like a tree that reaches over to get water or sun even though a tree can barely move. It felt strange that he should be lying right next to me feeling so much hunger when I was so content and so full. I couldn't understand how he could need so much and not see how perfect everything was.

Then after a while I heard Barb moving around and I knew she was getting dressed to go. And when she left I could tell that she took part of Mitch with her. I could feel it go, and I could feel how different he was without it.

I opened my eyes and I could almost see the skylight

and I could hear the rain on the skylight, but without my glasses I couldn't see any rain. I had to imagine what it might look like. I had to know in my gut it was still Pearl.

Then Mitch blew out the candle but it was okay. She didn't go away.

It was perfect.

I know I was only five, and I know I'm not supposed to remember so much so clearly. But it was a real moment, the start of something, and it's etched in. I don't even care whether anyone believes I could remember so much, because I know I do. Maybe the words or details changed in the remembering, but I don't see that it matters, because the words and the details aren't what's important, and what's important didn't change.

CATHERINE RYAN HYDE

MITCH, *age 25*: **what pearl left behind**

I pitched into the following morning underslept, over-stressed, underlaid, and really in no mood for Cahill.

He showed up at ten after nine. Took one look at me hobbling around on my taped-up ankle and howled with laughter. Cahill was always good for a laugh at my expense.

"Oh, geez, not again," he said. "Another rough night on the battlefield of love? I swear one day I'm going to have to bury you after that woman is done with you. That little size four commando. Geez, Doc."

Conversationally, he was getting harder and harder on Barb, heading for a line I was not about to let him cross. I didn't know exactly where it was, but somewhere near; we could both feel it approaching. The day previous he had called her "Mrs. Stealer," and when I corrected him and said it was Stoller, he said it was merely a matter of tense.

I'd almost jumped in his shit right then, but that wasn't quite the line. Just close.

"Jump off it, Cahill."

He picked up on a tone.

"Ooh. My mistake. Maybe somebody didn't get laid after all." It irritated me that both of his supposed shots in the dark had fallen right on target. "So, why is Leonard still here?"

"It's a long story."

Hannah chugged in at nine-twenty, still halfway doing her hair. "Morning, Doc," she said. "Morning, Cahill. Morning, Leonard. Wait. Leonard?"

She didn't ask if he had come early or stayed late because he was still in his little couch bed, in my T-shirt, with his glasses off, stretching and rubbing his eyes.

"It's a long story," I said.

Graff rolled in significantly after ten. Like this was news.

"Graff," I said. "You're late. Even for you."

He sighed, rolled his eyes. Hopeless is the best word I can use to describe Graff. "Got a fucking ticket."

"Language," I said.

"Oh. Sorry, Leonard."

"Speeding again?"

"California stop. You know. Rolling stop at a stop sign?"

Cahill's head came up. He rarely paid attention to Graff except to tease or express irritation. "We know what it is, Graff. Hey. Here's a thought. Maybe Doc can get that ticket fixed for you. He's got an in at city hall. Or is that a bad choice of phrasing, Doc?"

Graff, with his usual aplomb, said, "Huh?"

"Graff, Graff, Graff," Cahill said. "Are you so blissfully, eternally out of the loop that you actually don't realize that Doc is boffing the mayor's wife?"

Hannah caught my eye and then looked away. Leonard was tucked safely—and, I hoped, out of earshot—in the far corner playing a computer game. It was designed for first graders, but he was a smart kid. I hoped he was concentrating hard.

Graff said, "Oh." He looked a little confused. "Nobody ever tells me anything." Another painful silence. Then he said, "Oh, yeah. She was in here a while back. Nice-looking woman."

"Yeah, she's a real catch," Cahill said. "If you happen to have a hard-on for your grandmother."

Ah. The line.

I walked over to Cahill's chair. Spun him by both shoulders until he was sitting facing me with a look of mild surprise. I took two good fistfuls of his shirt and pushed his chair back until his head hit the glass of his monitor with a solid thunk.

"Ow," he said, reaching back with one hand to rub the spot.

"We're friends here, Cahill." The flat coolness of my voice surprised even me.

"Right," he said. "We are."

I still had him by the shirt, a point clearly not lost on him. "Do I treat you with respect?"

He rolled his eyes. Tried to stand. I pushed him back again, and his head thunked the monitor again. He held still, looking away like a belligerent schoolchild. "Usually, yeah."

"So, have I earned your respect in return, then?"

"Yeah. Okay. Enough."

I thunked his head once more on purpose, just to underline the point. "Then don't ever give me less than my due. Okay? Get the hell out of here if you can't act like a friend."

I let go. Stepped back. He rose to his feet, and we stood almost nose to nose for an awkward length of time. Maybe the count of five. You could hear the silence radiate. Even the Avian Americans were quiet. I could feel my teeth grind together. In my peripheral vision I saw Leonard's head pop up over his computer.

I waited for Cahill to hit me, or for me to hit him.

Then he took a step back. Brushed off his shirt like I'd left germs on it. "Fuck you, Doc," he said, hit the door, and kept going.

I breathed it out a minute, then looked around.

Everybody was staring at me. "Business as usual," I said. I sat down and pretended to get back to work. Really I had no idea what was even on the screen in front of me.

After a few minutes of this Hannah brought me a cup of coffee with a generous splash of half-and-half. She put her hand on my shoulder, tentatively, not sure if I would bite. When I didn't she said, "Doc? Is Cahill coming back?"

"Fuck Cahill," I said. "Oh. Sorry, Leonard. Cahill can go work for somebody he respects."

"Want me to finish the account he was working on? I think it's kind of ASAP. That new appliance store downtown. We promised to finish their Web site by Friday. I think that's the day they run ads for their big sale."

"Yeah, thanks. That would be good."

The whole room began to breathe around me again.

I got up and took my coffee and walked over to where Leonard was playing his computer game. I put one arm around his shoulder, and he stopped playing and looked up at my face and then let his head drop back onto my arm.

"Sorry you had to hear that," I said.

"What's boffing?"

"Oh. It's, uh . . . something you don't have to worry about for a long time."

"But it's something to worry about?"

"Well," I said. "It's not supposed to be. But everybody *I*

109

know worries about it. How are you doing on this game? You like it?"

"Yuh," he said. "I found the worm three times."

For the first of many moments, it struck me as touching that he hadn't asked when his mother was coming to take him home.

About ten-thirty that night, I was sitting staring at the TV in the dark when Cahill came back. I hadn't locked the door yet. He stuck his head in.

Leonard was asleep on the couch beside me, and Zonker was perched on the armrest, playing with that weed-hair and occasionally stroking the side of his beak against Leonard's face.

If you'd asked me what I was watching on the tube I couldn't have told you. Actually it was just an excuse for staring. I'd just been staring all day, since the rest of the guys took off, a longneck beer sitting on one leg, sweating through my jeans, the cold neck tilted in my hand.

"What?" I said.

"I *am* your friend, Doc. I'm the best friend you got."

"I'll cultivate enemies," I said, but I didn't put much behind it. All my wrath had abandoned me, leaving me stunned and tired and mildly drunk.

He came in, slamming the door too hard behind him. I looked down at Leonard, but he didn't wake up.

"I'm down on her because I want you away from her. I want her out of your life."

"Let's take this in the kitchen," I said. "I got a sleeping kid here. I just got him to sleep."

Cahill looked down at the little lump on the couch. "Holy shit. Leonard is still here? Isn't she ever coming back for him?"

"Let's take this in the kitchen," I said.

I hobbled in behind him. While we were in there I got another beer.

"You have any idea how old she is, Doc?"

"I don't care. Get your mind on another track."

"I think you do care. I think you care plenty. So tell me. How old is she?"

"Like . . . I don't know. Mid-thirties."

"You don't even know."

"And you do?"

"Her fucking biography is on the Web site we designed for the mayor's office."

"I didn't do that part."

"I know you didn't. I did. Forty-two. Four-two." My stomach went cold. Don't be a jerk, I told myself. It's just a number. "And you do care. You know as well as I do this is a dead-end street. I mean, I've seen some guys lose it over love, but you take the prize, Doc. Look what she's doing to you."

"What's she doing to me? She makes me happy."

Cahill let out a snorting sound, spun around, walked to

111

the other end of the kitchen, banged his head on the wall, and walked back. Like he had all this energy and could not contain it in the face of what I'd said. "Happy?" he said. "Happy? How many minutes out of every week is she making you happy? Look at yourself, Doc. Look what's happened to you."

"I have no idea what you're talking about. You want a beer?"

"When we started this business—"

"We?" I said.

"Okay, when you started this business and I got in on the ground floor with you, we did all kinds of shit. We went dancing. Hung out with girls. Got laid. You were a fun guy. You cared about all kinds of things. You cared about this business."

"I still care about this business."

"Do you, Mitch? Do you really? He's the biggest account we've got. The biggest account we've ever had. What do you suppose he's gonna do when he finds out—"

I heard a little noise from behind him. "Mitch?" Leonard was standing there pulling the elastic strap of his glasses into place behind his head.

"Shit," I said. "Now you woke up Leonard."

Leonard said, "I was sleeping but then you guys yelled. Why are you yelling?"

Actually, I hadn't known we were. I'd thought we were exercising a certain restraint. "Sorry, buddy. Just working some stuff out. Come on. I'll put you to bed." I carried him back to the couch, trying to limp as little as possible, and tucked him in.

"Whatcha watching?" he said. I had no idea. I looked up and a mummy lumbered across the screen in black and white. "Monster movie," he said. "Cool."

"You going to get scared if I let you watch?"

"Prob'ly, yuh."

"Just a few minutes."

Cahill was standing in the corner near the birdcage. Looking out at the street. He looked lonely. He looked as if he'd lost his best friend.

"If you felt this way, Cahill," I said, "you should have come to me and spelled it out like you're doing now. Not sniped it out in front of our co-workers."

"I realize that," he said. "I know that now. I'm sorry."

We all just stood our ground quietly for a minute. Zonker had found his own way back to the cage. Pebbles reached out and picked at a seam on Cahill's shirt, but he didn't seem to notice. The mummy came back on-screen and Leonard cupped his hands over his glasses.

Cahill said, "So. Do I still work here?"

For some strange reason, for just an instant, I felt something hard at the back of my throat like maybe I wanted to cry. "Nine a.m.," I said. "Be here or you're fired."

He walked over to the couch and stuck his hand out to me and I shook it. Then Leonard stuck his hand out to Cahill and Cahill shook that, too. Then he let himself out.

Leonard said, "Are you guys friends?"

I said, "Yeah. We are."

"Even when you yell at each other?"

"That's the best way," I said. "If you can yell at each other and still be friends then you know that's a real friend."

"Oh," Leonard said. "I didn't know that. I don't have friends. Except my mom."

"How can you say that, Leonard? You've got me. And Cahill, and Hannah and Graff. And Barb. And Zonker."

"Oh," he said. "Yuh. That's right. I got a lot of friends now. Don't I, Mitch?"

"You got 'em coming out of your ears," I said.

The following morning I knocked on Mrs. Morales's door.

"Who is that?" she said through the peephole.

"Mitch Devereaux. Your next-door neighbor? I wanted to ask you about Pearl."

"I think she lied to me about her name," Mrs. Morales said. "I think she was in trouble. She got arrested. Driving my car. I didn't know she didn't have a license. They called me, asked if she had my permission to use the car. Pearl

Somebody, they gave me her name, but the last name was not the same as she told me. I forget what they said. I backed her up. Maybe I shouldn't have, but I did. She was a nice girl. Even if she was in trouble. She kept this place so clean. I wish she would come back. Already it's beginning to go to seed."

We were standing in the upstairs room she rented to Pearl and Leonard.

"I'm sure she'll come back," I said. "I just want to get some of Leonard's things."

"I hope so. My dishes are stacking up. You could eat out of that sink when Pearl was here." She fretted her way down the stairs and disappeared.

I made my way around. It was a tiny unit that I think had been two bedrooms once, now illegally converted to a studio with kitchenette. Spotless, like she said. The bathroom was only a half. She must've bathed Leonard in the sink. And herself? I didn't want to know. It was none of my business.

I still fully believed she would be back. At least I think I did. So I didn't want to snoop. But then I thought about what Leonard said. How they were going to move someplace new. A whole new state. Orrington, I think he called it. I got a sudden all-over chill. Maybe Pearl just moved on without him. But she wouldn't do that. Would she? She adored that kid. Then again, what did I really know about her?

I gathered up two pairs of pajamas with feet, three

shirts, some tiny underwear and socks, a stuffed giraffe from the one small bed.

I opened the closet. I just had to see.

Hanging on a few of the bare, mostly abandoned metal hangers were two dresses, a faded blouse, and a pair of jeans. And it was impossible to guess if this was all Pearl had left behind, or if this was simply all she'd ever had.

## LEONARD, *age 5*: **the cuss jar**

I remember I was at the kitchen window talking to a bird.

I was supposed to be eating my breakfast, but I took my toast to the open window, and crumbled up little bits of it and set them on the windowsill. This little sparrow was diving down to share my breakfast with me. If I just stepped back from the crumbs and very quietly said, "Come on, Pearl, it's okay, Pearl," the little bird would come.

I never used to call my mother by her name. I always called her Mom or Mama, like any other kid. But after she left I started calling her Pearl, and I don't even know why. But the name Pearl is special. It sounds like a treasure, like a gem. Something you're all delighted and surprised to find, every time. Like when Mitch took me to the beach and the sun was going down, and the waves hit the rocks and threw splashes of ocean up into the air, right in

117

front of the sun, and it looked like somebody—God maybe—took a big handful of diamonds and threw them up in the air, just to watch them sparkle. Except actually, that happened later, after I got my better glasses. But anyway. Like that.

And, by the way, I think that was Pearl, too.

Mitch came into the kitchen and asked what I was doing and I said I was talking to a bird.

"Good conversation so far?" he asked.

And I said, "Yuh."

Just then Graff yelled, "Shit!" in the other room, and Mitch and I said it together at exactly the same time.

We said, "Cuss jar."

Everything was quiet for a minute, and then we could see him through the kitchen doorway, standing at the fishbowl, digging in his pocket. "Damn it," he said. "This is getting expensive."

Then everybody laughed at once except Graff and he had to put in two dollars. We made a lot of money off Graff. Every day. Everybody else got smart pretty fast and held on to most of their money.

When I looked up, the little sparrow had flown away. But that was okay. Pearl came to me all the time in all kinds of ways, all kinds of different things. Candle flames and rain and little birds. But when it stopped raining, or Mitch blew the candle out, or the bird flew away, I never felt that she was gone.

It was such a great thing. It just filled me up.

Mitch said there was a lady coming to talk to me that afternoon, to make sure I was okay.

What lady? I wanted to know, and why would she think I wasn't okay?

He said that any time a little boy is away from his mother there are these people who work with the government who come check on that little boy to make sure he's doing okay. He said it was up to this lady whether I stayed here or not, so if I was happy here, which he figured I was, I should tell her so.

"Okay," I said. "I'll tell her. I'll tell her I got friends coming out of my ears."

He said later, after she was gone, if I wanted, we could cash out the cuss jar and go do something fun. Whatever I wanted.

I could always use that money for anything I wanted. Toys or games, Mitch said. It was like an apology to me for bad language. I usually didn't buy toys. I liked to use it to take Mitch places, like out for lunch or an ice cream or to the movies. I didn't think Mitch was really all that happy, and I wanted him to have more fun.

"How did she know I was even here?" I wanted to know. I never talked to the government myself, and it was hard to picture Mitch having a conversation with it, either.

He said Mrs. Morales had talked to the police and asked them to look for Pearl.

"Oh," I said. "I don't think they'll find her."

Mitch seemed real interested and kind of worried that I said that. I had no idea why he was making such a big deal about it. He kept asking me why I would say that. Did I know something he didn't?

I wasn't sure how to answer that question. It seemed like a complicated question. I told him I might know some things he didn't, but I didn't really know all of what he knew, so it was hard to say for sure.

Then he spelled it out a little better and asked if Pearl had told me where she was going before she left, and I said, no, she hadn't said anything.

"Well," he said, "then why do you think the police won't find her?"

I said, "I just don't think they'll look in the right places."

I didn't know all that much about police, but I knew a little. I knew enough. When was the last time you saw them look for somebody in a raindrop or a candle flame or a splashy wave or a little sparrow?

## MITCH, *age 25*: **love my wife**

Harold Stoller's house consisted of thirty-five rooms on four acres. It sat smugly on a hill overlooking the ocean on one side, the lights of the town on the other. The guy had made a killing in my chosen field, computer software, only sooner, and better, and it showed. A valet parked my ratty, rusting Volvo, and I made my way to the door in my only good suit, and the silk tie Barb had given me as a gift when I complained I didn't even own one to wear for the occasion. And with Leonard draped snoring over my shoulder. I'd dressed him in his newest, cleanest pajamas and wrapped him in a decent-looking blanket. Under the circumstances, what else could I do?

I knocked, and a maid in a black-and-white uniform opened the door. I was thinking, this place is so bizarrely surrealistic. Nobody really lives like this, right? Or, if so, why?

"Mitchell Devereaux," I said.

"Yes, come in."

I was standing in the foyer, wondering what to do next, when I saw her. Wondering whether to ask the maid what to do with the kid. Wondering whether it would be decent and proper to slip the maid a few bucks to find him an inconspicuous place to sleep. I couldn't just walk into the mayor's dinner party with Leonard on my shoulder. Could I? But what if he woke up in this strange place and got scared? Then Barb strode out of the kitchen and stood at the end of the long hall, looking at me. Her hair was done in a rather fetching, not-too-conservative style, and she was wearing a snug, fitted dress that looked almost like a long suit jacket. And she was wearing those legs. She started down the hall in my direction, and the maid disappeared, and I wondered if, when she got to me, I'd still be able to put ten intelligible words together into a sentence.

She took the two steps up to the foyer, where I stood frozen. Talk, I thought. You have to.

"I'm really sorry about this. Hannah was supposed to babysit but something came up. She called me barely half an hour before I was supposed to leave. I couldn't get anybody else on that kind of notice. I didn't know what to do. I couldn't just miss this. I didn't know what else to do."

Talk, I thought. Don't babble. There's a difference.

She put her hand on my sleeve. "No worries," she said. "We'll fix it. Come with me."

I followed her up a carpeted staircase and along an upstairs hallway. She rapped quietly on a closed door, and we waited there for something to happen. I thought I could smell her shampoo from where I was standing and I wanted to reach out and touch her hair, but I didn't.

A heavy, middle-aged Hispanic woman opened the door. Over her shoulder I saw that her TV was on. She'd been watching something that looked like a soap opera on a Spanish-speaking station.

"Marta," Barb said. *"Quiero que el niño duerme en tu cuarto. Vamos a pagar extra, no te preocupes. Si tienes problema, dime."*

*"Sí,"* Marta said. *"Sí,* Missis, okay."

Marta accepted the limp parcel off my shoulder and laid him out on a daybed, tucking the blanket around him and running the backs of her fingers over his cheek.

*"Gracias,"* Barb said.

*"Por nada,* Missis. Is okay."

Then we were standing out in the hall together, completely alone. She looked me up and down as though she'd never really seen me in the light.

"God, look at you. You're so handsome. I've never seen you in a suit before."

I said, "It doesn't happen every day."

"Nice tie."

"*I* like it."

She gave me a smile that made me want to pull her off into the upstairs bathroom and get her out of that great dress. Or just work around it, I didn't care. She reached out and removed the handkerchief from my breast pocket and brushed at the shoulder of my jacket with it.

"You had a little bit of drool," she said. "It's okay now." She refolded the handkerchief and tucked it back in my pocket.

"I'm sorry about this." I gestured with my head in the direction of Marta's quarters.

"It's taken care of. Forget it. Slip Marta a twenty before you go."

I made a mental note to slip her two twenties.

We turned and walked down the hall together. Back to the land of the guests. And Harry. It came back down on me like an anvil on a cartoon mouse. I felt like I was walking to the gallows for my own beheading.

On our way down the stairs I felt her hand run down my sleeve and touch my hand. She gave it a quick squeeze.

"Relax, Mitchell. It's going to be fine."

Then we were downstairs and it was too late for any of that. No more room for the slightest touch or the most subtle aside.

It was time to be received by the mayor.


"There he is," Harry said. Bellowed would be more like it. "Come here, you."

He was standing out on the deck on the coastal side

with three other people, all of whom were strangers to me. The sun set behind a sharp line of fogbank just under his left armpit as he held his arms outstretched. He had a drink in one hand, which, come to think, might be the only way I'd ever seen him. I thought he wanted to shake my hand, but he threw his arms around me and gave me this great smothering bear hug, which startled and embarrassed the hell out of me. I could feel a little of his drink slosh onto the back of my jacket.

Then he held me at arm's length and looked me over. "You look great," he said. "You look like a young man on his way up. Which is exactly what you are."

Harry was a fleshy, beefy man of fifty-something, with silver hair and leathery skin and a made-to-order political persona. When he smiled I could just see that face on an election poster. I wondered how much he had spent on those teeth. Nobody is born with anything that perfect. I pictured his dentist driving an imported luxury car.

"Let me introduce you around," he said. "This is Martin Broad, my campaign manager. And a damn good one he is, too. And you've met Bruce Stagner."

"Of course," I said. "Mr. Stagner. Of course." I had no memory of ever having met the man.

"And this," Harry said with a great flourish, "is my daughter, Karen." He reached out for her and swept her around by her elbow to face me.

"Your daughter," I said.

My face felt flushed and I prayed it wasn't obvious. In

front of me stood this stunning woman who looked maybe a year or two younger than me, with butt-length hair, a tight, off-the-shoulder dress, and cleavage that just wouldn't quit. I knew their daughters were grown and out of the house, but I'd been seriously wishing for a pouty college freshman.

Harry said, "Come on, gentlemen. Let's give the young people a chance to talk." I hoped like hell he didn't mean that the way I knew damn well he did.

"Well," Karen said. She looked down into her cocktail glass, absently twirling an ice cube with one long, red fingernail. "The famous Mitchell."

"Why am I famous?"

"Mom and Dad think very highly of you. Dad says you're a talented young man. And he told me you were handsome, too. He didn't exaggerate. Hard to imagine somebody hasn't already snapped you up."

If I had, at that moment, fallen through the redwood decking to my death, it would have come as a welcome alternative.

I didn't, though. I'm sorry to say I didn't.

Over dinner Harry dropped the news. Clinked his knife against his water glass until all eyes turned to him.

Then he said, "I suppose you're wondering why I called you all here."

Barb was seated right across the table from me, and I shot her a look, which I had been trying to avoid doing.

Then he announced his intention to make a run for Congress. "It's a long shot," he said. "I'm a one-term mayor, and not of the biggest city in California. But it needs to be done. There's been a three-term Republican stranglehold on that seat. Some good, middle-of-the-road Democrat has to come along and break it. Maybe I'm the guy who can do it and maybe I'm not. But I've got great people on my team, and that's what counts. That's where all you competent folks come in."

He went on a good bit longer. Everyone stared with rapt attention, and so did I, but I wasn't listening. I was thinking, if he wins they'll move to Washington. Then I thought, no. If he wins he'll spend eighty percent of his time in Washington and she'll still be here. I wondered how long it would take me to find out.

I wondered if Leonard was sleeping peacefully.

I felt a foot bump against mine, a small woman's foot. I thought it was Barb, connecting with me under the table. But just at that moment Barb half-stood to move a floral arrangement, because it obstructed a guest's view of the mayor as he spoke. I knew her feet had to be underneath her.

As she leaned forward, the vee of her dress lapels spread slightly and I found myself looking down her dress. Move your eyes, I thought, but I couldn't. I couldn't look away. My body reacted to the sight of hers, and I couldn't convince it that this was not the moment. It wouldn't listen to reason.

Karen was, of course, seated next to me. So my search for the owner of the foot needed go no further.

The rest of the guests were long gone. I ached to be but had not succeeded in making my break. Instead I had been railroaded into the parlor for a private game of pool. I puffed lightly on the illegal Cuban cigar that my host had insisted I smoke. He'd also brought me a brandy from the wet bar in the corner of the parlor, and it sat on the rail of the pool table, mostly untouched. I was driving for two that night. But I sipped at it occasionally for his benefit.

"This is a real opportunity for you if you use it well," he said. "There'll be expansion involved. You'll need new hardware, new employees. You'll work closely with Marty Broad, and also with Barbara. She'll be coordinating. We're talking Web promotion, direct mailing, publications, electronic communications, the whole nine yards. Everything computer related goes to you."

He also said some other things I missed while I was thinking, how did I ever get into all this? I never intended to do software or Web design or have my own business. I wanted to teach grade school. It seemed weird to remember that, like it was decades ago. But really that dream was just a few years stale. I'd come to this town for college. Got my teaching degree and then got distracted by money. You don't exactly get rich teaching grade school. But I don't think money mattered at the time. And I couldn't remember when it started being about the money. Why it suddenly mattered.

But Harry was still talking, and I was missing it. Of course, drunk as he was, he was probably missing most of it, too.

"There'll be some late nights involved. You can't handle it all, delegate. But it's still your baby. Barbara, she knows how I want things run, and she can be places I can't. But I know you two can work together. She thinks highly of you. You know that, right?"

"I have a great deal of respect for the woman, sir."

"That's good," he said. "You know. Love me, love my wife. That sort of thing."

"I do, sir." Then I quickly added, "Both." It dawned on me gradually that I had just told Harry I loved him.

"Don't call me sir." A wave of his hand sent a plume of exhaled smoke rolling over the table. It wrapped around the hanging Tiffany lamp and clung there, only slightly swaying. "Makes me feel like a dinosaur. You know you can call me Harry."

"Right. Of course. Harry. I'll need to make a fairly early night of this."

"Of course you have good people already," he said. I'm not sure he'd even heard me. "You have that good assistant. That sharp young man. What's his name?"

"John Cahill."

"Right, right. And look. If I get elected, there's a bonus in it for you. Substantial. You know what I mean when I say substantial?"

"I don't think I do, sir. Harry."

"I mean walk into a Mercedes dealership, pick one out, pay cash. That kind of substantial. A man on the rise needs a good car. Show the world who he is. Where he's going."

"Don't think I don't appreciate it," I said. "But I'm thinking I need to make an early night of this."

A movement in the hall outside the parlor caught my eye, and I looked up. Barb was crossing the doorway, hesitating just long enough and just wickedly enough to really take me in, and I returned the favor. She smiled, and then the vision was gone again, leaving me tingling, hollow, disoriented. Half erect and completely stupid.

"My daughter seems quite taken with you," Harry said. He clapped me on the shoulder, startling me. I tried to line up a shot. "You have no idea how much it would please me to welcome you into this family in a more literal sense."

I watched miserably as I scratched the cue ball into the side pocket. "Your shot, sir. She's a lovely young woman, but that might be a bit premature."

He fished out the cue ball and placed it rather drunkenly on the green felt. Once again I had no idea if my words were even getting through.

"I never had a son," he said. "Wanted one, though. Oh, I know. I'm being mushy. Forgive me. I just want you to know that Barbara and I care a great deal about you." For one awful minute I thought he might be about to cry. How many drinks has he actually had? I wondered.

"I'm honored," I said. "Really. But I should be going."

He clapped me on the shoulder again and racked up a new game. We hadn't yet finished the old game, but I didn't correct him.

She walked me out to my car. The valet had apparently gone home for the night.

I buckled Leonard into the passenger seat and slammed the door as quietly as possible. Then I turned to face her and leaned on my car. We just stood for one long, quiet moment in the dark. Alone and free for one wonderful split second of time.

"What are you going to do about him?" she said.

"Who?" I thought she meant Harry.

"Leonard."

"Oh. Well. I don't know. What *can* I do?"

"I mean, if she doesn't come back."

"Oh, God," I said. "I can't think about that now. Please don't make me think about that now."

"Okay. Sorry." She reached out and touched my face for just a fraction of a second. We both looked up at the house. Every window seemed to face out onto the spot where we stood. She let her hand fall again.

I said, "That was really, really, really, really awkward."

"You were fine, though," she said. "You did fine."

"He stopped just short of telling me I was the son he never had. I had no idea he felt that way. I mean . . . does he? Does he really like me that much, or did he just have a little too much to drink?"

A barely perceptible shrug. "A little of both, I think."

"If he wins are you moving?"

"No. He'll just be away a lot."

Wouldn't that be a shame? I wanted to say. But I couldn't bring myself to. I couldn't shift gears that fast. I was still too unbalanced. It would have felt too callous.

"Maybe Tuesday," she said. "He'll be out of town. I might be able to stay the night. I'd have to put my private phone on call forwarding. You'll have to let me answer your phone if it rings."

"Does he know?"

I'm not even sure what possessed me to ask. But it had flitted through my mind at several points in the evening. I'd felt almost like he was driving at it.

Love me, love my wife. You'll have to work closely with Barbara. There'll be some late nights involved. I know you two can work together.

It felt like a system of hints. It felt calculated.

"Dear God, no," she said. "If he ever knows, you'll hear about it. Believe me."

LEONARD, *age 5*: **i knew that**

Hannah bumped me off my regular computer, the one I played games on while the rest of the guys worked. As Mitch liked to say, I'd graduated quickly from the first-grader games and moved on to using a joystick to save the universe by repelling alien invasions.

"I gotta have the seventeen-inch monitor this morning," she said. "Here. You can use the old laptop."

She set it on my little desk. The guys actually gave me my own desk. How cool is that?

"But it doesn't have my games installed."

She held up a disk. "I put 'em on floppy for you. I got you all set up."

Then she started working. But she was talking to me at the same time, trying to explain how to find my games on the A drive. I knew I wasn't going to be able to do this,

133

but I couldn't quite figure out how to tell her. The screen was just too little.

"Double-click 'my computer,' " she said.

"I don't know what that is."

"The icon that looks like a little computer."

"I can't find it," I said.

"Upper left of your desktop."

"Oh. Okay." I could see icons, just not well enough to know if they looked like little computers. I double-clicked the one in the upper left corner. I was just trusting Hannah. "Now what?"

"Now hit 'three-and-a-half-inch floppy A.' "

"I don't know where that is."

"Leonard," she said. "You know an A when you see one."

"Yuh," I said. "But I don't see one."

She stopped what she was doing. Saved and closed the file I think. Then she came and looked over my shoulder. "You don't see an A anywhere on that screen?"

"Not really."

"Okay, come with me a second. Let's try this on the seventeen-inch."

She popped out the disk and put it into my regular computer. "Try it now," she said.

I double-clicked the little icon that looked like it was a computer. Then I said, "Oh. There it is. A." I had to lean in a little, but I could see it.

"Is that why you lean in so close?" Hannah asked. "To see the screen better?"

"Yuh. Why'd you think?"

"Gee, I don't know. I thought you were just being intense. Well, never mind," she said. "You can have the big computer. I'll work on the laptop for now."

A minute later, when Mitch got off the phone, I heard her say, "Doc? Can I talk to you privately for a minute?"

MITCH, *age 25:* **the pledge**

The optometrist said, "Amblyopia in the left eye. I can't help noticing that."

I said, "In English, please?"

And Leonard said, "It means my eye wanders around. Looks at my nose a little too much."

The doctor laughed. "Why do I think this is not your first eye appointment?"

"Because it's not," Leonard said.

"His prescription has changed a lot. Too much, really. His myopia is progressing pretty rapidly. That's why I strongly suggest a dilated exam with an ophthalmologist. Too bad we don't have more information about his background. He wasn't by any chance a premature baby, was he?"

"What in God's name would that have to do with anything?"

"There's an eye disease related to prematurity—"

"Yuh," Leonard said. "ROP. I got that. From being borned too soon."

I just kind of stared at him. Wondering why he'd never told me. Then again, I suppose I'd never asked.

"Well, that fills in a good amount of background, right there," the doctor said. "He should be screened every six months or so to prevent later complications."

"Yuh," Leonard said. "I know."

"What kind of complications?" I wanted to know.

"Well," the doctor said. "In ninety percent of retinopathy of prematurity patients, the symptoms seem to reverse themselves without intervention. But in the other ten percent there can be serious complications. The scar tissue can cause retinal dragging, which I suspect may already be coming into play. Sometimes growth in the eye through adolescence causes retinal tearing. Or actual detachment. What we call late-onset retinal detachment. That would be the worst case. That's what we're screening to prevent."

"And the upshot of that would be . . ."

"If left untreated? Blindness. But there are excellent treatment options. I'm sure a good ophthalmologist will discuss them with you. Of course, you not being the actual parent, I'm not sure how much of this you want to know. But if you're legally fostering him, the state of California might be some help to you. If you're willing to brave the red tape."

"So, we're talking expensive."

"At this point," the doctor said, "I'm not sure you even want to know."

We were driving home in the car, and he had on his new glasses. He just couldn't get over how cool they were.

"They're so light," he said. He was shaking his head back and forth, then up and down. No elastic strap, either. The light lenses helped keep the glasses from falling off. Also the doctor had fitted the earpieces so they wrapped around his ears from behind and held on. He could hold his face down with the glasses pointing at the floor, and they weren't heavy, and they didn't fall. I knew this was the pair of glasses Pearl had always wanted him to have. Thing is, they were expensive. Really expensive.

"Now I can play games on the laptop," he said. "Now I can play with Zonker and not get Pebbles by mistake. Are you sure you could afford them, though?"

But I was somewhere else completely. "What?"

"Are you sure they didn't cost too much?"

"Don't even worry about that. Just enjoy them."

"Yuh," he said. "I do. Already. Mitch? Does Bar like me?"

"Well, of course she does. Everybody likes you. You're Leonard. How could anybody not like Leonard? I mean, what's not to like?"

"Know what the best thing about these glasses is? I can see Pearl in a lot more places."

I opened my mouth like I was about to say something. I think I was about to ask what the hell he was talking about. Then I closed my mouth again and didn't even bother.

She had me flat on my back, half draped across me. I was trying to get my breathing back. Maybe Cahill was right. Someday when she was done with me I'd end up six feet under. I still figured I was getting a good deal.

When I could breathe enough to say it, I said, "When I dreamed about the time you would actually sleep with me . . ."

"Yes?"

"I thought there'd be some sleeping involved."

"You can sleep tomorrow night." I got the impression that she thought we weren't done yet. I tried to think of a polite way to correct her. "I need a drink of water," she said.

"Don't go yet," I said. "Don't go for a minute."

"Why not?"

"I don't know. Just don't."

I rolled on top of her and held her for a minute, up on my elbows to spare her the bulk of my weight, the full length of our bodies pressed together.

Somehow I never seemed to end up on top. Well, not never. But not often. Only in the most intense states of abandon. And she always had to go when it was over. If only to get a glass of water. Somehow I thought it could be different just this one time. Somehow I thought we were breaking new ground, or that we could, if I just pushed a little harder. But I doubt I had admitted all that to myself at the time.

She ran her hands through the back of my hair for a moment. Kissed me on the forehead.

"Minute's up," she said. "I'm thirsty."

She rolled me off her, threw back the covers, and stood. I lay with my hands clasped behind my head, taking her in. Thinking this night would last weeks if it had to. I hoped it wouldn't have to.

The moon was strong that night, one or two days before or after full. I was amazed she would stand there in front of me naked in so strong a light. She had ways of avoiding these things.

Then she grabbed my red corduroy shirt off the chair back and put it on. Maybe she heard me thinking. Maybe she saw me taking her in, memorizing her to hold in store for the lean times, like those survivalists with six months' worth of dried food secreted away in the garage. Maybe she just liked to wear my shirts. I had this theory that it was her way of getting closer, getting into my skin, but safely. Of course that theory supposed that she wanted more of me, so perhaps it was too optimistic. But somehow I don't think so. There was another level to her. Just because she didn't give it away for free didn't mean it wasn't under there somewhere.

"Don't kill yourself walking around down there," I said.

"I nearly did, on the way up here. What is all that stuff?"

"We're cleaning out that extra room. That storage room. It's all going into a rented storage space, and then we're going to fix that room up for Leonard."

She was buttoning the shirt as I explained this, but she stopped. Just stopped with a button in one hand and a buttonhole in the other, freeze-frame. Then the film began to roll again, but I knew I'd seen what I'd seen. I wanted it to go away; I wanted to think it meant nothing, to forget it. But it didn't feel like something destined to go away on its own.

She walked over to the window, opened one slat of the blinds, and peered out, kind of aimlessly, not like she really expected to see anything. A band of light from the street-lamp fell across her face; her hair was beautifully disheveled, that just-ravished hairstyle.

"Why?" she said.

"Boy should have a room of his own. Besides, it makes his social worker happy."

"Why should he have it here, though? He's not your boy."

I didn't answer right off. I fought a coldness inside, almost a mild shock. I remembered Leonard's voice when

141

he asked me if "Bar" liked him. I think that was the first moment I realized Leonard knew more than I did. The first of many, believe me.

"Why *not* here?" I said.

"Why not? Think, Mitchell. Think where you are in your career. Think of all the responsibility that's just been laid on your shoulders. Who do you think told him you could handle it? This is a hell of a time to suddenly decide to become a single father."

"I can handle it," I said. "You told him that because you knew it was true."

"I don't think you know what's involved in parenting."

"I'm sure I don't," I said. "But I can handle it."

She just stood there, staring through the blinds at nothing. The tension in the room felt palpable, as if it might materialize into some recognizable form at any moment. In a calm, dispassionate sense, this was a fight. We'd never had one, and I hadn't seen this one coming. Leonard had.

"I'm not sure if *I* can," she said.

"What?"

"I think you heard me."

"What are you saying?"

"I'm saying I raised two of my own, it was damn hard work, and I feel I've earned the right not to hassle with kids anymore."

I swung my legs over the side of the bed. I was headed up and across the room in her direction, but I realized I was angry, and I didn't want to come off as aggressive as I felt. I didn't want to come at her that way. So I just sat there on the edge of the bed, naked, trying to fathom what had shifted between us.

"You act like you fucking live here," I said. "What could you possibly have to hassle with? You come in the middle of the night, you stay an hour or two, and you slip away. He's asleep when you come and when you go. I should be so lucky that you're here enough to be burdened by my actual life."

"I'm sorry you feel that way," she said. She took off my shirt and dropped it on the floor, then gathered her own clothes and began to dress. I knew she was leaving, and I felt deeply cheated, because just this once she was supposed to have stayed the night. "If this is falling so short of your expectations, you should have told me."

"Oh, Christ, Barb, don't. Don't do this. I can't believe you're leaving."

"Well, I am," she said. "Believe it or not."

I had the awful feeling that she was leaving in a more permanent sense. That she was telling me this was it. It was over. I sat there watching her dress, thinking of a dozen different ways to ask, but none of them panned out right. No matter what the phrasing of the question, I sensed the danger that she might answer.

"Give me some time to think about this," she said and headed down my ladder-stairs for the door.

I just sat frozen for a moment. Then it struck me that

she was leaving, really leaving, and I had so much more fight in me. So much to ask, so much to say.

"Barbara!"

I yelled it out, risking waking Leonard. Then I hopped around trying to get both legs into my jeans at once. No answer. I suddenly felt as if my sanity depended on not letting her get out that door. Then I heard the door snap shut. I took the ladder two steps at a time, a kind of Russian roulette for a broken leg, but it worked. I ran to the door, threw it open again.

"Barbara!" I shouted again. Then silence.

I stood staring out into the moonlight. I couldn't even see which way she had gone.

"Damn it!"

I slammed the door hard, then kicked it even harder. Not toes first, I'm not that stupid. Kicked it with the flat of my foot, leading with my heel. But I didn't feel any better, so I threw my body against it, yelling "Shit" at the same time, then slid down into a sit with my back against the door. Everything had drained out of me, there was nothing left to kick, and I didn't feel one bit better.

I looked up to see Leonard sitting up on the couch, with his new glasses on, watching me.

"Mitch?" he said. "What happened, Mitch?"

"Nothing. Nothing happened."

"Yuh, it did."

I promised myself I would never thoughtlessly, automatically lie to him again.

"You don't have to put anything in the cuss jar for that," he said. "I understand."

I lay on my back on the bed with just my jeans on, with Leonard by my side.

"Light a candle?" he said, and I did.

He curled up against my arm, hugging it the way an adult hugs a whole human being, a kind of miniature spoons position. "Thanks," he said. "I'm sorry you're sad."

"It's okay."

We were quiet for a while, and then he said, "Do you know what forever love is?"

"I don't think so." I couldn't really think. But if I had been able to think, I don't think that would have helped. I think I really didn't know.

"Pearl taught me. It's when you love somebody so much that no matter what happens that'll never change. Like even if you're gone. It's still the same. Even if you die. You die, but not the love. Not forever love. Know what I mean?"

I thought he was trying to refer to something between me and Barb, because that's where my head was, and in that context, no, I wasn't sure what he meant.

He reached out and put his hand on my chest, feeling around for a heartbeat. Pearl must have done this with him, I thought. A kid this young doesn't make these rituals up on his own. Or does he? I wasn't sure.

When he was sure he had my heart, he held his hand still, and it felt warm against my skin. "That's how much I love you, Mitch. Okay? Do you feel better now?" Then a second later he said, "I didn't mean to make you cry, Mitch."

"No, it's okay. It's a good thing. Thank you. Thanks for the forever love. It helps."

"Yuh," Leonard said. "I know."

When I was sure he was asleep, I reached for the phone. Managed to inch over slightly to get it without disturbing him.

I dialed her cell, because I knew she couldn't be home yet.

Two rings. She answered by saying, "Hello, Mitchell." Then, "Just got him back to sleep, did you?" We were both silent for a beat or two, and then she said, "I guess I don't understand why you feel the need to keep him."

I could feel the weight of him on my arm. The candlelight flickered across us and made us look like all part of the same being somehow, a complex but single organism. I wondered if I could answer without crying again.

"I'm lonely," I said. "Can you understand that?"

Silence on the line and I thought maybe I'd lost her, in more ways than one. Maybe she'd gone out of range.

"Of course I can," she said at last. Her voice sounded soft. Softer than usual. "I just can't fix it for you."

Then the connection broke up, and I lost her completely, so I clicked off the phone and just lay there, hoping she'd call back. But of course she never did.

I lifted Leonard's new glasses away from his face, carefully angling the earpieces off from around his little ears. I held them up to the candlelight, to see them better. The lenses were clear, new, unscratched. So light compared to the old ones. So much more like what he deserved. I set them on the bedside table and watched him sleep for a while.

He'd put his hand on my heart and vowed to love me forever. And all I'd done was taken him to an optometrist and bought him a decent pair of glasses. I still owed him big-time.

After a while I blew out the candle and rolled in his direction. Threw one arm over him so I was more or less hugging him back.

Forever love.

I said, "I pledge you back, buddy." That probably wasn't fair, to tell him while he was sleeping, but at the time it was what I was able to manage. I said, "You're not going blind on my watch, buddy. Not if I have anything to say about it."

Before I could even finish the last sentence, I'd fallen back into wondering what all this was going to cost. In any number of different currencies.

\* \* \*

The moment she walked in the door of our little work-place, everybody fell quiet.

Nobody knew she had been "gone," not really knew. Except me, and possibly Leonard, though we hadn't discussed it out loud. But there was some kind of tension in that room, she'd brought it in with her, and it ran through everybody like electricity, and nobody made a sound.

Cahill made a point of trying to catch my eye, and Hannah made a point of avoiding it.

My stomach felt all cold and shocked inside, a kind of prehistoric flight response, and I was thinking how awful it would be if she had just come on some business-related matter, and wasn't feeling one bit warmer toward me. I knew this was when I would find out if it was really over. I felt dizzy.

She strode through all that silence with her confidence intact. Came around behind my desk and put her hands on my shoulders. Very quietly and close to my ear, she asked if she could speak to me privately for a moment. We took it in the kitchen. The loft would have been a lot more private, but it's my bedroom, so that might have seemed a little weird.

I leaned back on the counter, and she came within one step of me. I could smell her perfume and her shampoo. Please don't let this hurt, I was thinking.

"How can you not like Leonard?" I said. I thought it was brave of me to just come out with that.

"I do like Leonard. Of course I like Leonard. He's a great kid. How could anybody possibly not like him?"

"That's what *I* wanted to know."

She glanced over her shoulder to the open kitchen doorway. "Do they know enough not to come in here?"

"Absolutely," I said.

And she walked right in and put her arms around me. Rested her head on my shoulder. I held her in return, strangely aware of my hands on her back. Strangely aware of my breathing. I worked at swallowing but it wasn't the usual piece of cake. I actually had to work at it.

After a while she lifted her head and pressed her cheek against mine. It put us nearly ear to ear. "I don't want it to be over," she whispered.

I tried to say something back, but it was all such a jumble inside me. Trying to find one single thing to say was like trying to unwind fifty feet of tangled rope without any backtracking or hesitation.

"I can't go back to the way it was before I met you," she said. "I can't. I need this."

I tried to pull my head back, to look at her, but she stopped me. Stopped me with one hand on the back of my head. "No," she said. "Please. It's hard for me to say things like this. So don't say anything and don't look at me, okay?"

A moment of silence which must have passed as my

assent. It had to. I wasn't allowed to say anything. Her body, pressed up against me like that, was driving me insane. Not even so much a sexual thing; there was too much on the line for that. It just drove me to get even closer, like I could climb inside her skin and lose this damn separateness that threatened to implode me.

"I've been behaving like a spoiled child," she said. "And I just hope you can forgive me. I still think you don't know what you're getting into, but it's your business. I reacted the way I did because . . ." Breathe, Mitch. Swallow. Don't say anything. "I guess I was enjoying being everything in the world to you. Don't even say it. Don't even tell me how selfish and unreasonable that is. I know. I'm sorry." A long moment of her breath against my ear. Then she said, "You're not saying anything."

"You told me not to."

"Oh, that's right. Well, say something."

But that was harder than it sounded.

I wanted to say, Well, you're human. Imagine that. I wanted to say, How incredibly wonderful that you were jealous. I wanted to say, You're back, nothing else matters. I wanted to say, My God, you actually told me something real.

But I never got the chance. Just then we heard Cahill's voice bellow in from the front room. I had never heard Cahill say anything so loud.

"Hey! Marty!" he shouted. He sounded like he might have learned the voice from Harry. "Marty Broad! How ya doin', Marty?"

Barb jumped back a step and I let my hands fall.

I heard Marty say, "Uh . . . I'm fine." Obviously confused by Cahill's enthusiasm. As anyone would be. Anyone who knew Cahill knew he had no enthusiasm.

I looked up, and Leonard was standing in the kitchen watching us. I thought about all the things he might possibly say in front of Marty.

I made a mental note to have a serious talk with the kid.

LEONARD, *age 5*: **what love isn't**

Later that evening, when everybody was gone, Mitch said
he wanted to talk to me. It sounded kind of serious.

"Yuh," I said. "Okay."

"It's very important," he said, "that you never talk to
anybody about Barb. About seeing her over here, about
anything that you might see while she's here. You
must never tell anybody that she's here at night.
Especially never say anything in front of Harry or Marty
or anybody from Harry's office, but I think the best
way to not make a mistake with that is to not say anything to anybody at all."

"Cahill and Hannah and Graff already know," I said.

"Yeah, they do. But they know better than to say the
wrong thing to the wrong person. And I just want to make
sure that you do, too. Do you understand?"

"No," I said. "But I won't say anything."

"What don't you understand?"

Why would love be a secret? That's what I didn't understand. It was pretty confusing. But I didn't really want Mitch to explain it to me. I didn't really want to talk about this anymore.

All I asked was, "Is it wrong?"

He breathed a lot, and didn't answer for a minute. "I'm not sure how to explain this," he said. "They would think it's wrong."

"Who?"

"I don't know. Anybody."

"But it's not?"

"It's complicated," he said. "Maybe somebody could even get hurt. But I can't say I think it's wrong."

"But everybody else would."

"Some would," he said. "But you won't know who would and who wouldn't until it's too late."

I thought maybe if almost everybody else thought something different than me, I might think they were right and I was wrong.

"Someday when you get older, you'll understand," he said. "For now, I'd appreciate it if you'd just go with me on this."

"Yuh," I said. "Sure, Mitch."

I wasn't looking forward to talking to anybody about anything so confusing ever again.

### LEONARD, *age* 17: **what love isn't**

I still remember my first lesson about love. Not forever love, but the other kind, the kind people use every day. The kind that only works with grown-ups. The kind that always seems to self-destruct after a while.

Really it's the opposite of forever love when you think about it. It's more like a time bomb, and the only real question is how the clock is set. How long it will tick before the explosion.

I walked into the kitchen one morning while Barb was in there with Mitch. I knew she was in there, too, and I think that's why I walked in. She had just come back, after that time when I'm pretty sure Mitch thought maybe she never would.

In one way I knew they wanted to be alone in there, but in another way I could feel their intensity rolling out of the kitchen like waves. I could smell it, the way something heating on the stove sends its good smells out to the people in the living room, and makes them want to come and get it.

I just had to go in.

Mitch was leaned back on the counter, and she had her arms around him, and her head on his shoulder, and they both had their eyes squeezed shut. Then she picked up her head and put it near his, so their faces were touching all along one side.

I knew they were saying quiet things to each other, but they must have been really quiet, because my sense of hearing is great.

I could see his hands on her back, and there was something hungry about them.

I couldn't stop watching, and I couldn't stop wondering, if this is love, why does it look like it hurts?

But it really looked like love, to the point where I couldn't imagine what else it could be. It was so intense. I figured it was just a kind of love I'd never seen before. So I waited to see Pearl in it, but she wasn't there.

Funny, I thought. They both seemed so sure. Just for a minute even I got fooled. But it was not the real deal. It had failed the simple test.

Then Marty came, and Cahill said his name real loud from the other room, and they jumped apart like they'd been caught doing something wrong. So, right there it failed another basic test. How could love be something wrong? Why would you need to make sure anybody didn't see it?

Then Mitch looked up and saw that I was standing there. And even though I could see that he minded me less than he minded Marty, he seemed uncomfortable.

It was all very confusing at the time.

Years later I developed the simplest litmus test of all. And found the simplest possible way to communicate it. If it takes you apart, that's not love. Love puts you back together.

Eventually I even shared this theory with Mitch, though of course I approached the whole topic as reverently and sensitively as possible.

But, predictably, he had no more understanding of my theory than he might have if I'd explained it all in Latin.

Long-term complications of retinopathy of prematurity. Laser photocoagulation. Cryotherapy. Late-onset retinal detachment. Scleral buckling surgery. Retinal dragging and folds. Vitreous surgery. International classification of ROP. Injection of intraocular gas. Retinal reattachment surgery. Blindness.

Blindness.

Blindness.

The worst thing about my list of new words, other than the actual retinal detachment part: it was laced with treatments that could have helped Leonard already, at earlier phases of the game. Except blindness, of course. That was a specter for further down the road.

Leonard remained absolutely silent on the way home from the ophthalmologist's. Maybe he was freaked out, but I doubt it. He'd heard all this before. I was the one learning the new language. I was the one with the words spinning in my head. And behind each new word, more words. Hidden words. Words like insurance coverage. Pre-existing conditions. Hospitalization. I was the one who was thrown, and I fully believe he stayed quiet only to allow me time to think.

There are screening programs for ROP in most neo-natal intensive care units. That's what the ophthalmologist had said. They screen because so many of these problems can be avoided with early diagnosis and treatment.

Well, then, what happened? I wanted to know.

Well, she'd said. I don't know. I wasn't there. But if the mother was on public assistance, or was just low income . . . if she had to resort to a county hospital. I hate to say it, but it's a factor. I can't sit here and pretend it's not a factor, she'd said. And when the condition was diag-nosed, even if the mother had Medi-Cal, well, just try getting Medi-Cal to throw for laser photocoagulation. Since there was no guarantee that he was headed for more than pronounced myopia. They'd probably buy him a cheap pair of glasses and leave it at that.

I remembered the first phone conversation I'd ever had with Leonard, remembered him telling me he had to spend lots and lots of time at the clinic. What clinic? I wondered. How good a clinic? What did they really do for him? Everything I would if I had my way? Or just the least required? Just what Medi-Cal would throw for?

Visual rehabilitation. Flashes and floaters. Traction retinal detachment. Slit lamp biomicroscope. Ophthalmoscope. Ora serrata. Arteriovenous shunts. Neovascular ridge.

The orbiting words were beginning to give me a headache.

"Hey, Leonard," Hannah said when we got back. "How was your eye appointment?"

"Fine," he said.

"Come over and sit on my lap and tell me about it."

"He might have a little trouble finding his way there," I said. "He's dilated."

Leonard carefully felt his way around the desks until he found Hannah's. Then he sat in Hannah's lap, as requested, perfectly cheerful as always. "It went fine," he said.

I wondered how much he'd had to memorize the lay of this place already, just with his old glasses. It was impossible for me to fathom what it meant to be that nearsighted. What adjustments he made. How his life was different from mine. What the world looked like to him.

"So, what did the doctor say about your eyes?" Hannah asked.

"Oh, you know. Same old stuff."

Cahill said, "So, Doc, want to see the results of the first campaign polls?"

"That depends," I said. "Will I like them?"

"That depends," he said. "Do you want the man to win?"

"Of course I do, Cahill. What the hell kind of question is that?" I owed the cuss jar a buck.

"Then, no," he said. "You won't like them."

Barb came back at ten o'clock that night. We made love for almost an hour, that desperate, clingy, incredibly satisfying make-up sex.

Then after an unusually long stay she rose and dressed, and I put on a robe and walked her to the door. At least, that's where I thought we were going. Instead she sat down on my couch, which—now that Leonard had his own bedroom—conveniently no longer contained any sleeping boys.

She asked if I had tea without caffeine. She said if she drank caffeine this late she'd be up all night. I put on a kettle of water and then sat down with her. I wasn't quite sure what we were doing. Whatever it was, we had never done it before.

"You can't really judge much by the polls," she said. "Especially not this early. A lot of winning candidates get off to a slow start."

"I don't know anything about the process," I said. "But I agree it's too early to judge."

"So," she said. "What's changed since I last saw you?"

"I'm sorry. What's the question?"

"I'm asking what you've been doing."

"Oh. Okay. Right."

That's when it hit me, what was happening. And I felt stupid for being so slow to understand. She was staying afterward to talk to me. To hear about my life. In other words, she was responding to my earlier complaint. I supposed that meant I had cut her with that complaint in some way. I couldn't have imagined, at the time I'd said it, that it hadn't gone without saying. But you never know when you're going to cut somebody.

"Well, let's see. We moved Leonard into his new bedroom. Found an office to rent downtown. We're outgrowing this space so fast. Cahill went to a bankruptcy auction and bought a bunch of new hardware. What else? Oh, and we took Leonard to get his eyes checked out."

The kettle began to whistle, and I got up to get it.

I made her a cup of herb tea, then got a little vague on how she might want it. I didn't know whether to steep it dark for her, and I didn't know whether she took honey or sugar. That struck me as sad. I felt I should have known that about her. I decided I would just have to ask.

But she wasn't where I had left her on the couch. I looked in the downstairs bathroom, but the door was open, the light out. I climbed the ladder to the loft, stuck my head over to look, but there was nothing happening up there.

When I came down I saw the door open to Leonard's

bedroom. I walked by the doorway slowly, hesitating only briefly to look. He was still fast asleep, and she was standing in the dark by the edge of his new bed, her back to me. I felt like a thief trying to steal a piece of that moment, whatever it was, so I went back into the kitchen. Put the mug of tea on a tray, with the jar of honey, and a saucer for the tea bag, and a spoon. She could sort the whole thing out the way she wanted it.

When I got back out to the living room, she was sitting on the couch as though she'd never left. "Thanks," she said. "Let it steep awhile." She leaned against me, so her back rested against my chest. I wrapped an arm around her waist. "So, what was the upshot of his eye exam?"

"Long version or short version?"

"Just the gist of what it adds up to."

"He has this eye condition that premature babies sometimes get. There are good therapies for it, but they're expensive. You have to have either money or good insurance. On Pearl's income I guess they were more or less out of the question. Anyway, at this point he's a good candidate for tearing in his retina. He'd have to have this cryotherapy technique to repair it, and then they might have to put a silicone band around his eye to reshape it. To get the retina to lay flat. Otherwise it could lead to complete retinal detachment. Even if he gets through childhood without too many problems, when he's a teenager the scar tissue in his eyes could tear the retina. Because the eye has grown. If it isn't repaired, and fast, he might go blind." We sat without talking for a minute, her hand stroking my bare wrist. "I'm beginning to see your point," I said. "About biting off more than I can chew."

"Well, you've made the choice, so you'll live with it. You'll make the best of it. You can handle it as well as anyone. What are the chances that you'll actually be keeping him permanently? Are you planning to try to legally adopt him?"

I had talked to his social worker about this at some length. Problem is, she'd said, they favor two-parent homes. If a good two-parent adoption home comes along, well . . . Anyway, she'd said, not all kids get so lucky, so we'll wait and see.

"That could go either way."

"Well, it's a coin toss, then. Maybe this will all be your problem and maybe it won't."

"I know I shouldn't ask this, but I can't help it. I have to. What were you doing in Leonard's room just now?"

Silence radiated for a moment. I knew she would have preferred I hadn't seen, and I felt again that perhaps I should have kept the question to myself.

"Just telling him I was sorry," she said.

Barb and I had a lot in common. All of my most noble moments with Leonard happened while he was sleeping, too.

★   ★   ★

After she left for the night, before I went to bed, I let myself into Leonard's room and sat on the edge of his bed.

I thought for a while about what I would do if someone adopted him. If they were responsible and had financial options, fine. They could see to his eyes. But if they didn't do it, or didn't do it right, it was still my problem. Because I'd promised him that if I had anything to say about it he wasn't going blind. That was one problem. The other problem was that it hurt, already, to think about him living with somebody else.

"I'm really glad Barb came back," I said. "But I hope you notice that I didn't sell you out for it. I'll never sell you out."

Then I decided this was unfair, and it had gone too far. In the morning, over breakfast, when I was sure Leonard was awake, I would tell him that I'd love him forever, that I wouldn't let him go blind if I could help it, and that I'd never sell him out.

A boy deserves to hear these things while he's awake.

## LEONARD, *age* 17–18: **preflight check**

I'm waiting for a special moment. It's exactly three minutes away. It's three minutes to midnight in the driveway of my adopted parents' home, and at midnight I will be eighteen. And when I'm eighteen I will be no one's responsibility but my own. And nobody can tell me where to live or what to do. And it's only three minutes away.

There's a good, strong moon tonight, and I'm sitting beside my finished craft, waiting. Waiting to belong to myself. I love my adoptive parents. I really do. But it doesn't feel right to belong to them. They're great people, really, but they are not Pearl, and they are not Mitch. And they are not me.

I've backed Jake's truck into the driveway, nearly up to the glider, and it's just sitting there. The truck and the glider and I are all just sitting here, quietly.

Jake has this truck that he uses in his construction trade.

It has one of those metal racks across the cab and bed, from bumper to bumper, a raised metal rack for strapping down lumber and such. Gliders and such. I bought a huge tarp, because no matter how tightly I lash it down, no matter how slowly I drive, I'm afraid of the wind getting underneath it, and lifting it up, just the way it's designed to do. I'm afraid if I'm not careful the whole truck could fly. Well, not literally. But it might be hard to control.

Okay. It's time now. It's time. I belong to me.

I manage to lift and position the glider across the rack of Jake's truck. It's light. It sticks out way too far, crazy far, both front and back. But the streets should be more or less empty. If the cops or the highway patrol spot me, it's probably over. But I don't have that far to go.

I tarp it all around and lash the tarp down to the truck in every possible direction, to every possible tie-down. At every tarp grommet, I find something to secure it to. Front bumper, back bumper. Tie-downs in the bed. Problem is I have to leave plenty of room for the wind to get under the front of the thing, because otherwise the tarp would obstruct my view of the road.

It's okay. I'll drive slowly.

I go back into the kitchen and leave a note for Jake. Tell him I'm sorry I lied about the crash helmet and the additional ground school, which I think I've had plenty of already and Jake doesn't, and the fifty air hours before I launch off a cliff, and the professional inspection on the glider, and all the other things I promised. I tell him I'll be as careful as I can under the circumstances, and I'll be back. No guarantees, actually, but probably I will be.

I tell him if for any reason I don't see him and Mona and the other kids again, please know I love them all and I'm grateful for everything they've done for me. I tell him if I do come back I'm going back to live at Mitch's house, which should not in any way undercut that love and appreciation. It's just that Mitch and I need each other in a special way, like one of those jagged-cut playing cards in the spy movies, that two people fit together to make sure they've got the right match.

Then I tell him that if anything should go wrong, his truck will be on the bluffs at the end of that long dirt road across the railroad tracks. I'll leave the keys in the magnetic key holder under the driver's side wheel well. Mona can drop him off to get it, or actually he could really walk or bike there if he wanted. It's only a few miles.

I coast out of the driveway, all silence, lights off. Then I let the truck drift down the street. At about the corner I turn the key and it sputters to life. I turn the lights on and I'm gone. Only about ten miles per hour, but I'm gone.

So this is what it feels like to belong to yourself, I'm thinking.

I could get used to it.

★   ★   ★

I'm up on the bluffs in the moonlight when I realize I've made one tactical error. Taking Jake's truck. Belonging to oneself carries a great many new responsibilities. Okay, on the one hand I lied to Mitch, I lied to Jake and Mona. I'm about to do something they all want me not to do. But I can do what I want to. What I need to. I'm mine. But Jake's truck is not mine. That's a different matter. I can't just take what isn't mine.

I know I have to adjust the plan.

I off-load the glider, which is wonderfully light but a little hard to handle. Balance is important and a little tricky, especially the way the wind gets underneath. I lash it to a telephone pole, retarp it. If nobody steals it, it will still be here when I get back. I've tied it down too tightly for the wind to upend it or take it away.

I sit on my haunches on the very edge of the bluff for a minute or two. Looking out across a dark ocean. Looking at stars, which may or may not be looking back at me. There's a train just a mile or two away. I can hear the tracks buzz and ring with it. I wait until it's clattered by behind me. I turn only once to look. It's a shiny silver Amtrak passenger train. I wonder for a split second if any of the passengers are awake. If anyone saw a newly liberated eighteen-year-old man squatting on the bluff in the moonlight, and wondered what he wanted, who he was. What that big covered hulk might be, lashed to a telephone pole by his side.

I wish I didn't need it. I wish I could fly on my own,

like I sometimes feel I should be able to do. I'd like to just spread my arms and leave this bluff and head straight for that star, that one very bright star.

But first I have to take Jake's truck back.

LEONARD, *age 5*: **that which is caesar's**

The day I went to kindergarten, everything changed.

I was standing at the window in my new classroom, watching Mitch walk away down the street. And just for a minute, I thought I might cry. But I thought about Pearl, and that changed the subject. That kept me busy just long enough for another boy to cry. And for the teacher to make an example out of him. She made him go to the coatroom, which had suddenly become "the crying room," even though I'm pretty sure it was the coatroom before that, and I know for sure it was the coatroom later on. She told us he could come out when he could be a big boy, like the rest of us.

I decided not to cry at all.

Then the teacher gave us beads to string. The girl next to me found exactly three of each color, and strung them three matching ones at a time. I wondered who taught her to do that. I mean, I couldn't imagine she had been born wanting to do it that way. I picked whatever colors I felt like picking. I tried to string it so when it was done it would be like Pearl.

The teacher came around behind our backs, stood over us with that big shadow, and told the girl next to me that she had done it "right." And she told me my beads were "messy."

"Wrong," I said. "Bull," I said. "If there was a rule, you have to tell it before we start. You can't just come later and say there was a rule." How dare she call Pearl messy?

"This is my classroom," she said. "You will not talk to me that way. Who put those ideas in your head?"

"Pearl told me," I said. "Just now." I pointed to the last place I'd seen Pearl. The beads.

I got sent to the principal's office. And Mitch was called. Fortunately he hadn't left for his office yet, because he was told to come get me and take me home for the day. My very first day and I got suspended.

I sat on the bench outside the office and waited for Mitch to come. I could feel Pearl tucked into a little spot just below my ribs.

Mitch came, and he took me by the hand and asked to talk to my teacher. The principal went in and sat with her class, and then the teacher came out into the hall like she owned it. She looked at Mitch, and then at me, and then at Mitch, and then at me. Like she was trying to work something out in her head.

"What seems to be the problem?" Mitch asked.

"The problem," she said, talking real slow like an actress on a stage, "is that this little boy has a rude mouth and a bad attitude."

Mitch's face totally swam, like he'd just been thrown into a pool and hadn't gotten back to the air again. *"Leonard?"*

"That boy," she said. "Right there." She pointed at me. "And another thing. I think he's just a little bit too old for that imaginary playmate. Don't you?"

Mitch just stood there with his mouth open, and then she stormed back into her room.

We began the walk home together, still hand in hand.

"Do I have to go back tomorrow, Mitch?" I waited until we were out on the street to ask.

"I'm afraid so. What happened in there, Leonard?"

"It's totally bogus," I said. "It's bull. And she's wrong. She's just plain wrong."

"Okay," he said. We stood waiting to cross the street because the crossing guard had gone home for the morning. "Here's a strategy for tomorrow," he said.

"What's a strategy?"

"A plan. You think she's wrong. But no matter what you say to her, she'll never think she's wrong. Never. The more you try to convince her, the harder your life will get. So try just knowing she's wrong, but protecting yourself by keeping that a secret."

"Okay," I said. "I'll try. Why did she keep looking at us like that?"

"I think she was trying to figure out how I could be your father."

"Why? Why couldn't you be?"

"Well, I can be," he said. "I am. But I think she was wondering about it because you're Asian, and maybe some other things, and I'm not any of those things."

"That sucks. You can be my father if we want."

"I agree," he said. "But get used to it. What was the bit about the imaginary playmate?"

"I just said something about Pearl is all."

"Oh."

"Bad idea, huh?"

"Probably. Just try it my way. If it still doesn't work, and she gives you a hard time again, you tell me, and I'll go down there and kick her butt for you."

"Thanks, Mitch," I said. "You're a pal."

173

## LEONARD, *age* 18: that which is caesar's

The day I went to kindergarten, everything changed. I learned the real opposite of love. That strange ringer love I saw in Mitch's kitchen may have been the opposite of the forever in forever love. But on my first day of kindergarten, I learned the opposite of the love. I became two people that day. Began to exist in the world without being any real part of it. As they say, render unto Caesar that which is Caesar's. Render unto God that which is God's.

After the nasty coatroom incident, I looked up at my teacher, and I was filled with the strangest sense of warring hatred and pity. I thought about Pearl's face, looking down at me with all that joyful, welcoming love. And I knew this mean, angry woman never got any of that.

So, what do you do? What do you do when someone is deprived of the most basic birthright of every human child and then goes on to victimize others because of it?

Do you hate her or pity her or both? I sensed the answer was probably both. This was the first moment I felt the two parts of me emerge and begin to do battle. This is when I learned I would not be spending my whole life playing computer games at my little desk and feeding toast crumbs to manifestations of Pearl. There were more layers to this life thing, and they were far less perfect than I could ever have imagined.

After the nasty bead-stringing incident, I stood up and turned to face her, and the hate was bigger than the pity. Now that the victim was me.

"Wrong," I said. "Bull," I said. "If there was a rule, you have to tell it before we start. You can't just come later and say there was a rule."

"This is my classroom," she said. Oh, so that's what this was about. Ownership. Power. Control. "You will not talk to me that way. Who put those ideas in your head?"

"Pearl told me," I said. "Just now." And for lack of a better direction, I pointed to the last place I'd seen Pearl. The beads. How dare she call Pearl messy?

Now I should interject here that I have never, since Pearl's death, actually heard her "say" anything to me. This is important, because I have many times been grilled as to whether or not I hear voices. I do not. I am not schizophrenic. Pearl doesn't talk to me. She doesn't have to. There is nothing more that needs saying.

It was more the chorus I heard when I looked at, and listened to, the colors of those beads. They resonated with something as real as the earth, as old as air. For a moment I felt sorry for that mean, angry teacher. Just for that moment the pity got bigger than the hate again.

It must be awful to be deaf and blind.

But, you know what? That was then.

Time to come back into the moment.

I coast up to the curb with the lights off. Gently pull on the hand brake.

I make sure I'm leaving the truck just the way I found it. I put the keys back on the hook in the hall, right where they always are. Then I go into the kitchen and take my note back. The truck is home, they know I love them, and, besides, nothing will go wrong. I'm coming back.

Moon Pie is awake, and he wants to come with me, and I let him. I get my bike out of the garage and ride it back up to the bluff in the dark. I can hear the puffing of his breath as he runs along behind me. I feel the wind whipping in my face, flapping in my shirt. This is how it will feel to fly, I think.

Only better.

## MITCH, *age* 37: happy birthday from pearl

It's about two days after my talk with Leonard in Jake and Mona's garage, in the shadow of his big bird, about two days after he showed me his tattoo and promised to follow every glider safety rule known to man.

It's about midnight.

I'm standing at the door of my neighbor, Mrs. Morales. I'm thrown back through the years to the last time I knocked at her door. Shortly after Pearl disappeared. I don't think life was honestly all that simple then, but it may well have been simpler than it is now.

I'm thinking about this as I wait for Mrs. Morales to open her door. I know it's too late, and I know I'm waking her, but it's her own fault for what she said on my voice mail. She told me to come over the minute I got the message. What was I supposed to do?

In time I hear a voice from inside. "Mr. Devereaux?"

"Yes, it's me," I say.

She opens the door and stands before me in her bathrobe, her hair flattened on one side by sleep.

"I apologize for the late hour," I say, "but I just now got your message."

"Come in, come in," she says and leads me into her dining room. She turns on the overhead light, an old-fashioned cut-glass chandelier. On the table is a small manila envelope, maybe five by seven. It looks old. Faded. Dog-eared. "Open it," she says. "Wait till you see."

My hands shake, wondering what could be so important. What this could have to do with me. But in another way I know, because only one thread runs through both of our lives.

While I'm working the clasp, which breaks off in my fingers, I hear her say, "I had that whole apartment remodeled. The workmen came in and tore out all the old wainscoting. They found this behind one of the boards. I don't know if one was loose, or if you can just pry one out. You know. If you need to badly enough."

I slide the contents of the envelope out into my hand.

Two birth certificates. One for Pearl Renee Sung, and one for Leonard Sung.

A strip of four black-and-white photographs of Pearl and Leonard, the kind you buy for a dollar or two at a carnival photo booth. Leonard is maybe three, with those heavy black glasses, smiling widely in all four shots, showing a complete absence of front teeth. Pearl is leaning her head on his in one. Kissing his temple in another. She looks worried and far away.

The last thing I shake out into my hand is a small pile of bills.

"Two hundred dollars in twenties," Mrs. Morales says. "Now I ask you. If she were going to ditch her son and run away, would she take off without her birth certificate and her traveling cash?"

"I don't know," I say. "I suppose not. I'm having a little trouble taking all this in."

"I'm telling you, something happened to that girl."

"That *is* beginning to look like the more reasonable scenario. You know what? Now that we know her name, we should check with the police. Maybe they know—"

"Forget it," she says. "I already tried. I've been on the phone all afternoon, ever since the workmen found that stuff. From the time I left that message for you to the time all the offices closed. There's no record she was ever arrested, and no record she ever died. It's weird. It's like she just disappeared off the face of the earth. It's like she just up and flew away, if you know what I mean. I'm giving you this stuff so you can give it to the little boy. You still know where the little boy is, right?"

"Of course," I say. "But he's not so little anymore. He'll be eighteen tomorrow." I glance at my watch and think, actually, he's eighteen now. And he'll be coming back to live with me. "He'll die when he sees this stuff. In a good way, I mean. The biggest regret of his life has been having no last name, no pictures of Pearl, and no way of knowing who his father was. Oh, by the way . . ."

I pick up Leonard's birth certificate. In the space for "Father" is typed, simply, "Mother refuses to state."

That's an odd thing to put on a birth certificate, I think. Don't they usually put "unknown" if they can't fill that space in?

Then I'm struck by a sharp image, a suddenly remembered impression of Pearl. And I know that if she knew who the father was, she wouldn't let them say he was unknown. There is shame in unknown. Unknown means you had sex with so many men you can no longer narrow it down. No, I can picture her making that point rather clearly with the hospital personnel. I know who the father was. You just don't get to know.

It makes me shiver for a moment because it's so Pearl. It brings her back so clearly. It's as if she were looking over my shoulder.

"This is going to be a hell of a birthday present," I say out loud. "A last name and pictures of Pearl. My God, that's two out of three of his life regrets wiped right off the map."

"I'm glad he'll get these things," Mrs. Morales says. "I feel so sorry for that boy. It's so awful to never know."

"First thing in the morning," I say. "As soon as I think he might be awake."

★  ★  ★

On the way home I glance at my watch. It's after twelve-thirty, but I'm tempted to go over there and wake him up. Let me be the first to wish you a happy birthday, I could say. But they have so many other kids, and Jake has to get up at six. It doesn't seem fair.

I actually cruise by, thinking maybe someone's light will be on. But the house is dark, quiet. The garage is closed up. Jake's truck is sitting in front of the house, just the way it always is. A few bikes lie on their sides near the garage. They're always there, and no one ever seems to steal them. It's such a placid scene.

I'll just come back in the morning.

When I get home I open a beer and sit looking at the contents of that envelope.

And I think, something really must have happened to Pearl.

Will he feel validated, because he's been trying to tell me that all along? Or is there a certain comfort in thinking she might be out there somewhere, somehow okay? The pure joy of sharing this with him becomes complicated with all these perceived emotional reactions. It will stir a lot of feelings in him. It has to. It's done that to me, and she wasn't even my mother.

For one split second I consider leaving well enough alone, but I quickly abandon the idea again. He's a grown man. Young but grown. This is his truth. It isn't mine to keep from him.

Maybe I'll take him out shopping, and he can spend the two hundred dollars and it will be almost like an eighteenth birthday present from Pearl.

That girl did have an eerie way of seeing to it that Leonard was always cared for. I never go to bed because I know I won't sleep.

I knock on the door, and Mona answers. Fortunately, Mona gets up early.

"Wanted to be the first to wish him happy birthday, huh? He's not up. He must still be in bed."

I go up to his room, knock. No answer. I push the door open. His room is empty, the bed perfectly made. No Leonard. No Moon Pie.

I find Mona in the kitchen, stirring a pot of oatmeal that looks as though it might serve twenty.

"He must be in the garage then. Working on that awful, dangerous thing we can't talk him out of."

"I'll try that," I say.

I walk into the garage, and it's empty. Really empty.

No giant dinosaur-bird craft.

No Leonard.

Just a shaft of early sun through the skylight, similar to the one that lit him so magically when I saw him last. This morning it illuminates nothing. A square of concrete floor.

How in God's name did he get that thing out of here?

One of my few comforts in the last couple of months was knowing that glider would be nearly impossible for him to move. He didn't build it to break down. What did he do, balance it on his back and ride off into the sunset with it on his bike? And no one was going to help him move it, because no one likes this idea one bit except him.

I sit on the concrete with my knees to my chest, my back to the garage wall, the envelope in my fingers. I close my eyes. I'm not sure why.

It seems like a thing with no real-world explanation.

It seems as though he's just disappeared.

It seems, for just a moment, that Leonard has simply up and flown away.

LEONARD, *age 7*: **things to get used to**

The day they took me away from Mitch I was seven. Nearly eight. And they didn't really take me away from him, so the joke was on them. I had to be big about it because Mitch was really upset.

"I wanted to keep you." He said that about thirty times that day. I told him I knew that, but I didn't make a point of the fact that he was repeating himself, because I wanted him to. I wanted him to always say it again.

"It's going to be okay," I kept saying. "We'll see each other a lot." It really wasn't that okay. It sucked. But I wanted Mitch to feel better.

Just before I got in the backseat of Jake and Mona's car, I pulled Mitch aside by saying, "I have to tell you a secret."

He took a few steps away from Jake and Mona with me. These total strangers that were suddenly supposed to be better because there were two of them, one male and one female. The way the world is supposed to work.

He leaned down so I could whisper in his ear.

"What's the secret?" I think he was about to cry.

"This is where forever love comes in really, really handy," I said.

Jake and Mona showed me to my room, which was on the second floor. Showed me around. The closet, where I could hang up my things, the half bathroom that was all mine. For the time being anyway. I was one of only three kids at the time. There was a dresser with a big wood-frame mirror on top. There was a baseball bat in the corner. I didn't play baseball. I hated baseball. Mitch would have known that.

"We'll just leave you alone to unpack," they said.

After they left I picked up the baseball bat and broke every pane of both windows. I broke the mirror over the sink in the bathroom. Then I picked up the big mirror off the dresser. It wasn't even bolted down. I threw it through one of the broken windows, splintering the wood frame. I heard it crash onto the driveway below.

I heard one of them running up the stairs.

I lay down on the bed and waited.

Mona came running in, and looked around, and then looked at me. She came and sat on the edge of the bed. Didn't try to touch me, which was good.

"You're angry," she said. "About having to leave Mitch."
It wasn't even a question.

"Duh," I said.


I had to go to a new school.

I was walking down the hall, minding my own business, when a foot came out from nowhere and tripped me. I went flying, and landed hard, and it knocked all the air out of me. My glasses went skittering off down the hall. The fourth pair of glasses Mitch had bought me. A present from him. Out of reach. I could hear them slide away. I couldn't see where they'd gone. Not without my glasses.

I heard a couple of kids laughing.

Then one of them sat on me. I literally couldn't breathe. I thought it was going to send me into an asthma attack, because a stressful thing like that sometimes will. I didn't know if my inhaler was still in my pocket, and I couldn't reach my pocket to see. I could still hear kids laughing.

I thought, where is a teacher when I need one? I wasn't fond of teachers as a rule, but I would have taken one right about then.

I thought, these people don't even know me. What could I possibly have done to bring this on? What can I possibly do to stop it?

I thought, is there *anybody* besides me whose mother

welcomed them into the world with a face full of joyful love? I mean, one single person besides myself?

I was going to have to breathe soon.

I wondered what Pearl would want me to do. The minute I thought that, I stopped struggling, and I stopped trying to breathe. I held still, almost like I was dead, so my need for air would be a lot less. I guess this bored the big kid who was sitting on me, because he got up and moved away.

I just lay there catching up with my breathing. It didn't go into an asthma attack, but I think it might have if I hadn't remembered Pearl. Then I felt a hand on my shoulder, and I heard a voice, a girl's voice.

"Here," she said and handed me back my glasses.

I put them on and looked up at her. Just an ordinary-looking girl, but I knew she'd gotten more welcoming love than most. "Thank you," I said.

I looked back over my shoulder, and there were four of them, and they were looking over their shoulders at me. And they were all bigger than me. I think that's when I first realized how small I really am. They were still snickering, and one of them gave me the finger. Then they turned the hall corner and disappeared.

I had never met them before, and already they wanted to hurt me.

I remembered Mitch's voice when we talked about being different races. I remember how he said, "Get used to it." I wondered if that would be his advice to me now.

## MITCH, age 34: we could just snuggle

On my fourth session with that therapist, she said this to me: "Whose problems are we here to work on? Leonard's or yours?"

It wasn't as sarcastic as I make it sound. It may have been a pointed question but I think she really was waiting for an answer.

"But that's just it," I said. "Don't you see? I blame myself for Leonard's problems. That's my problem. That I blame myself for his."

"You don't have one single one of your own?"

I think I just sat there with a stupid look on my face.

Her name was Isabel. She was about fifty. She wore her hair pulled back but not severely, and she wore skirt suits. I sat there watching her cross one knee over the other, listening to the way her nylons brushed together, and thought, did I actually not realize when I chose her how

188

much she reminded me of Barb? And how could I be so unaware of it then and so aware of it now?

Life's great mysteries.

"Here's an exercise for you," she said. "Here's something I think it might help us to do today. Think of something that's happened in the past year or so that really bothered you. That has nothing to do with Leonard."

"Okay."

We both waited for a moment.

"Oh," I said. "Right now?"

"Good a time as any," she said.

She never let me talk about what I wanted to talk about. That being the fact that I had failed that kid by never once initiating a dialogue about his missing mom. Well, that's not entirely accurate. She let me talk about it for three sessions. Then she felt it was time to move on to something else, but I didn't know what kind of something else she had in mind. I was still stuck on What was I thinking, not talking about Pearl with him, whether he seemed to want to or not? And anyway, that's about me. Isn't it?

I mean, this is not a healthy thing. Kid never once said, hey, Mitch, did you notice Pearl has been gone a few years now? What's up with that? And I never said a word intended to get him to open up about it.

I guess it takes guts to loose a spray of questions you know you can't answer.

Anyway, I wanted to tell Isabel how he's got this chip on his shoulder now with authority figures, and he's fighting at school and acting out all this rage at Jake and Mona, and it's all my fault.

But no. This woman with the legs won't let me talk about it, I was thinking. And it's the only reason I came. That and the obvious Barb comparison seem like reason enough to maybe ditch her and get somebody better. A guy would be nice. I could be headed for a heavy transference thing here. Like my life is not complicated enough. And it's not like we've been together forever or anything. It's only our fourth session. We haven't really bonded yet, I thought.

"I have something," I said. I guess maybe I expected her to be proud of me. Anyway, here's what I had.

Sometime going into that second congressional campaign, the one that worked, and put enough money in my bank account to hire this expensive therapist, I'd said to Barb, "Promise me you won't do one of those commercials. You know the kind I mean. The loving wife looks adoringly at her candidate husband while he looks into the camera and tells the voters how he'll keep their homes safe and let them keep more of their tax dollars in their pockets, which is exactly the same impossible drivel all the other candidates are saying but there's the wife beaming at him like it's some brilliant shit. Promise me you won't do that," I'd said.

"There you go again," Barb had said.

"There I go again what?"

"You know I can't promise that."

Somehow that wasn't what I had expected her to say. I thought I'd feel better after our little chat.

For a while we couldn't even talk about it without everything coming apart. Then we made a sort of truce in which I agreed that I would not watch the commercials. Which pretty much involved not watching television except late at night, which was the only time I really watched television anyway. When in doubt, look the other way. It's an acquired skill, but once you learn it, it's like riding a bicycle. It'll never really leave you.

But then one night, about a year previous to sitting in that dreadful session with the temporary Isabel, I was sitting home watching late-night television and they went into local ad time and there it was. Harold Stoller and his adoring wife for Congress. I wanted to turn it off, but it just froze me. It was too horrible to watch, but definitely too horrible not to watch. It had me.

For two days everybody I ran into said the same thing. "What's wrong with *you*?"

"Nothing," I said. Not in such a way that they would believe me, but in that tone that encouraged no further questions.

But here's what was wrong with me: Not even so much that the marriage could actually be real, a thing that existed and meant something, because I still didn't buy that. I was simply twisted by the fact that thousands would see that commercial and they would buy it. They would think that was a real marriage, an actual thing that existed and meant something, and even if I could find all those thousands of people who needed correcting, I wasn't allowed to straighten out the obvious misunderstanding.

The tiniest bit of denial. Perhaps. But that's what I felt.

Then after two days of my saying, "Nothing," she came to see me, and she let herself into the house and climbed into my bed at night, just like always.

And I found myself unable to perform. For what I think might have been the first time ever. We lay there side by side in the dark and I waited for what she would eventually say.

I believe the correct line is, "Don't worry, it happens to all guys sometimes." And then I think my line is supposed to be, "Well, it never happened to me before." But we never really scripted things out in quite the normal way.

A good two or three minutes must have gone by in silence. Then, finally, this was her big line: "You told me you weren't going to watch the damn commercials."

I wouldn't make a thing like that up.

So, I'm thinking this is the kind of thing this therapist person wants.

"Okay," I told Isabel again. "Okay. I've definitely got something."

We waited in silence for quite a long time. Patterns, patterns.

"Yes?" she finally said.

That's when it struck me that she wanted me to say all this out loud. I couldn't do that. I didn't even know her.

That stuff was top secret. I couldn't be telling it to just anybody.

"You said think of one. You didn't say I had to recount it out loud."

"Maybe next week we should talk about trust issues," she said.

But I figured by next week I could locate a therapist who would let me tell him that I blamed myself for Leonard's acting out. Whose money was it, anyway?

## LEONARD, *age 14:* **forever lenses**

I really had only one important private conversation with
Barb, but it was a good one. It took place after Harry won
his election for United States Senate. He blew that first try
for Congress, but he won the second time out, served
three terms, then set his sights on the Senate and moved
up big. This was part of what led me to my conversation
with Barb. Following a win like that, I knew Mitch had
money coming out of his ears.

I called her, and asked if we could meet. She didn't even
ask me why. Just gave me the name of a restaurant. She
handles life like a business. She trusted me to state my case
when we arrived. I guess she could deal with her curiosity
until then.

The restaurant was a little nicer than I thought it would
be. Not really fancy, but nice enough that I felt under-
dressed in my jeans and T-shirt.

She rushed in three minutes late, apologizing, and I apologized for not dressing up more.

"There's no dress code here," she said. "You're fine. Forget it."

She sat down across from me and really looked at me for the first time, and I waited for her to react to the state of my face. She just looked, nothing more.

"Are you hungry?" she asked. "Can I buy you lunch?"

I hadn't meant to get a lunch out of her in the package and I felt a little guilty. I had to keep reminding myself that she could afford this stuff. Where I come from, lunch out is a big deal.

"Why don't you just go ahead and say it," I said.

She looked up at my eye again, and her face got soft. She didn't say anything at first, just reached her fingers out so she almost touched it. Instead she touched a place on my cheek just below it. Right at the corner of my eyebrow there was an actual break in the skin, and a lot of swelling, and I'm sure it looked too sore to touch. And, as a matter of fact, it was.

"Mitchell told me you've been fighting at school."

I laughed. I guess maybe it sounded a little bitter. "That's what I tell him, yes."

"Whereas actually . . ."

"I'm getting the shit kicked out of me. Every day. Well, no. Not every day. But it seems like it. It seems like every time I turn around. Look at me, Barb. Who am I supposed to hold my own in a fight with? Do you have any idea

195

what I weigh?" I didn't want to tell her, so I just kept going. "Let's just say I'm about two inches shorter and twenty pounds lighter than the next smallest guy in my class. Then I have these big, thick glasses, and I walk around with an asthma inhaler in my pocket. I might as well be wearing a sign that says, 'Beat the crap out of me, I was born for it.'"

"Is this what you needed to talk to me about?"

"Yeah," I said. "More or less."

Then the waiter came and Barb said the veal piccata was really good here, and I reminded her that I was a vegetarian. She got a confused look on her face and said she hadn't known that, and then apologized. Like she damn well should have known it. The waiter said one of the specials that day was a vegetable lasagna with spinach and ricotta. I said that would be fine.

After he left I looked at Barbara like I'd never seen her before. I think I was appreciating her. "Thanks for buying me lunch," I said. "It's really nice." She just waved it off. "It seems amazing that you and Mitch have lasted all these years. Oh, shit. That was a really stupid thing to say, wasn't it? I'm sorry if that was a stupid thing to say. I should think before I talk."

"Forget it," she said. "It's okay. We're probably both a little surprised ourselves."

"It's just that there's always so much stress."

She sipped at her water. "Maybe it's the stress that holds it together," she said.

"That is *so* confusing." I held my head like it would come off otherwise. "That would totally give me a headache if I tried to think about it. So I won't." Besides, I already had a headache from being slammed in the temple with a locker door.

"How can I help with your problem at school?"

"I was hoping Mitch would buy me contact lenses."

"Of course he will. I know he will. All you have to do is ask him. You know that."

"Just one thing, though. He can't know I'm getting beat up at school."

"He's a big boy, Leonard."

"He can't. He can't know that, Barb. You can't tell him. I mean it. He hurts for me, Barb. He hurts when I hurt. Telling him I'm getting beat up would be like beating him up. I couldn't do that to him. I thought maybe it could be your idea. You could say, 'I bumped into Leonard today, and I was just thinking, wouldn't his social life be easier without the glasses?' And remind him it's not the kind of thing Jake and Mona's insurance would cover. But if you say anything at all, it has to be something that won't break his heart." We just sat with that for a moment, and then I said, "I'm counting on you not to break his heart."

I didn't literally add, "or you'll have to answer to me," but it was more or less sitting there on the table, obvious to both of us.

There was a quiet moment, and we were looking right at each other's eyes. I think we both knew, consciously, that it was a many-layered comment I'd just made. Most grown-ups wouldn't have let me talk to them like that. There were a lot of good things about Barb.

Then she nodded a few times, and I knew she was with me. At least on the contact lenses, anyway. "I'll make you a promise. Either I'll get the contacts out of him without him knowing why, or I'll buy them for you myself."

"Wow," I said. "You would do that for me?" I was touched. Really.

"Of course I would."

"Wow. That's really nice. You know, I used to wish . . . . No, you know what? Never mind. I think I've said enough stupid things for one day."

"Go ahead if you want," she said.

"I used to wish that you and Mitch could get married, and then it would be a two-parent home, and I could stay there. I knew you couldn't. Even back then I sort of knew. It's just one of those things you wish, you know? One of those stupid things that, when you're just a kid, you don't know any better than to want."

She smiled, but I knew I'd made her sad. But maybe it wasn't the worst kind of sad in the world. I don't know.

Later, just as we were walking out of the restaurant together, I told her I loved her.

She didn't look at me at first, then she did. I could tell she was trying to say something, and that she was really uncomfortable. And I don't think it's because she didn't love me back. I think she did. I think that was the discomfort. Right there.

"Thank you," she said. "You're very sweet." And she touched my face again and walked to her car.

I just stood there for a minute and wondered why that would be such a hard thing to say. What does it snag on, in some people, while it's trying to come out? What would it feel like to live inside that skin and not be able to let it flow in and out like that? I couldn't imagine.

I wondered if she had ever told Mitch she loved him. I knew damn well she did. In that strange, deficient way that seemed to be the only love she could manage, I knew damn well she did.

When I got home, there was a phone message on my bed. Mitch wanted me to call him. I called him at his office. He said he had a big bonus check, and he wanted to buy me a present. What did I want more than anything else in the world?

"Well," I said. "I've really been wanting to switch over to contact lenses."

"Done," he said.

He picked me up in a brand-new midnight blue Mercedes convertible. He took me out and not only had me fitted for contacts but he opened an account in his name with this eye doctor so all I had to do was go back anytime, be refitted for a fresh prescription, and the bill would go to Mitch. Forever lenses.

"Otherwise it wouldn't be a big enough present," he said.

That was an important feature, because I was still going to get beat up some, and I had no idea how long I could make a pair last.

I knew Harry had given him a bucket of money this time.

I called Barb and left a message on her voice mail. I said I wouldn't need her help after all, but I wasn't sorry we'd had the talk.

## MITCH, *age* 37: **flashes and floaters**

There are only two times I can remember Leonard needing me. Only two times he seemed really scared, and came running to me, wanting me to be a father to him. Most of the time he had this life thing aced. But there were these two times.

They fell a dozen years apart, almost to the day. Both times I was right in the middle of making love to Barb when he tapped me on the shoulder—literally or figuratively—to call me away. I suppose I was loath to be interrupted, both times. At the time I'm sure what I was doing seemed all-important. But, looking back, Barb let me make love to her hundreds of times. Leonard let me father him only twice. So I suppose it was worth the interruption.

The first time, he tapped me on the shoulder because he couldn't breathe. The second time it was because he couldn't see.

The phone rang, and I didn't care.

"Don't get it," I said. I was on the bottom, and she looked like she was about to get it. "Let it go," I said.

"My phone is on call forwarding," she said. "It could be Harry. I have to pick up."

Fortunately, by then I didn't mind the interruption nearly so much, because after the use of the word "Harry" things were pretty well dead in the water anyway.

"Hello," she said, still sitting astride me. Then, "Yes, he's right here, hon." She covered the mouthpiece with one hand. "It's Leonard," she said. "He sounds upset."

When I got to Jake and Mona's house, he was sitting on the porch in the pitch dark. At first I didn't even see him. There were no lights on in the house; the whole world was asleep minus two. Then I saw him making his way down the walk.

The two words he'd said on the phone still jarred around in my head. Flashes and floaters. Two big red flags of his eye condition.

"Leonard," I said when he got into my new car. "How long have you been having them?"

"The flashes a few days. Floaters around the same time. But tonight I was getting the curtain in my left eye, so then I got scared."

"Why didn't you tell someone?" My voice just kept rising. "Why didn't you tell me?"

I hadn't intended to shout. But the curtain. That meant the retina was actually detaching. The curtain was the retina itself, coming down. A painless descent into blindness. And speed was our only ally. And no one had told me until now.

Leonard sat very still, staring straight ahead. I wondered what he saw through those battlefield eyes. "Please don't yell at me, Mitch." He sounded like he was about to cry. Leonard never cried. That I knew of.

I pulled on the hand brake and threw my arms around him.

"I'm scared, Mitch," he said.

I wanted to tell him that I was, too. That all the shouting just arose out of all that scared. But nothing came out of my mouth at all. Even though I think I tried.

Leonard said, "I told Jake and Mona, and they put in for an authorization. They told Medi-Cal it was an emergency. But it's still not an emergency like a heart transplant or something. Anyway, we were still waiting. I didn't want to tell Jake and Mona how scared I was because it would be like I was in trouble and they couldn't help me. They were already so worried, so I didn't tell them when it got really bad. I called you instead. I'm sorry, Mitch."

He was dressed only in jeans and a short-sleeved tee and he felt so skinny and small.

I wanted to breathe some of my excess caring into him and make him big enough to take on any kid at school. I wanted to make him a big strong guy with perfect vision. I thought about the stories he told me, the way he made it sound like he picked fights at school. I wished he could trust me enough to tell me the truth.

I knew about the truth. I lived in the real world, with real bullies. When I was Leonard's age I was the fat boy. They beat the crap out of me. Everybody wanted a piece of me. Everybody got in my face determined to find and claim some last piece of dignity some other bully had overlooked. Strip it away, run it up the flagpole, and laugh as I stood shivering without it.

I took off my coat and put it around his shoulders. Then I made him put on his seat belt and we drove. God, how we drove.

After I sold the car I came back to the hospital, and Jake and Mona and I sat in the waiting room looking at our hands, then at each other, then back at our hands. Once I looked up at Mona and started to speak, but her mouth opened at the exact same time. We deferred to each other like nervous drivers at a four-way stop, each too polite to claim right-of-way. Then the moment was gone; whatever I had been about to say flew away and the room fell silent again. Well, actually it had never been anything but silent.

It was just the promise of some proper thing to say, like an oasis that turns out to be nothing but a mirage. It vanished back into desert.

"We appreciate it, Mitch," Jake said, startling me. I actually jumped. "Don't think for a moment we don't."

The "but" part just hung in the air, and everyone was careful not to look its way or do anything to encourage it.

Leonard was safely out of surgery, but still not awake. The doctors felt it had gone reasonably well, but we were all sobered by our entrance into the several-month period required to gauge the practical result. In a movie they would take off the bandages and Leonard would see. It was dawning on all of us, I believe, that this was not a movie.

"I know you wanted to be the ones to provide for him," I said.

"Doesn't matter," Mona said. "What matters is that he was provided for."

She was right and she was lying, all at the same time, and I could tell we all knew it.

"I know you wanted him to come to you when it got bad," I said.

The moment I said it, Mona burst into tears.

Jake moved over to comfort her, and gave her a handkerchief from his jeans pocket. A white cloth handkerchief. I'm not sure I'd ever seen one in real life. I'd only heard about them. I didn't know anyone really carried them anymore.

I watched Jake hover over her, trying hard to make it

right, and I felt wrong about myself. I watched his rough hands and pictured him coming home from hard days of labor, exhausted, while I drove around in my midnight blue Mercedes convertible, attending cocktail parties with the senator while I carried on a long-standing affair with his wife. Jake was a man who worked hard and did not deserve to be stolen from, and I worried that in some small way I had done just that. I had stolen his claim to father Leonard, not just on the night of his hospital admission but all along. I was complicit in a scheme to make him a father in name only, while Leonard and I held our bond in a secret pact, beyond the reach of everyone. And worse yet, knowing this, I wasn't quite willing to make it stop.

"What does he tell you about his troubles at school?" I asked. It seemed to come out of nowhere, even to me.

"He has trouble fitting in," Jake said. "He's small. He has glasses and asthma, so the bigger kids pick on him."

"He tells you that?"

"Of course he does. Why wouldn't he?"

I took a deep breath. "Because he doesn't tell *me*," I said. "He doesn't tell me. Because he thinks it would break my heart. Same reason he wouldn't tell you when he couldn't wait any longer for his eye surgery. He doesn't want to break anybody's heart."

Mona pulled a shuddery breath and blew her nose in the handkerchief. "People have to hear the damn truth," she said. "Heartbreaking or not."

"I know," I said. "I agree."

It hit me that when Leonard got out of the hospital it would be time to have a good long talk about Pearl.

The first time I got to go in and see Leonard he was lying on his stomach in bed, his face resting in a doughnut-shaped contraption to make the position slightly more comfortable. He had a thin hospital blanket pulled up to his hips. His gown was tied at the back of his neck, then fell open across his shoulder blades.

I asked him if he was cold.

Instead of answering the question, he swept his arms up and forward, and then back, as if swimming.

"Leonard Devereaux Kowalski takes the gold in the hundred-meter breaststroke," he said. Too quietly, I thought. It was too soon to joke but he was doing it anyway.

It was a thought out of nowhere, but it made me laugh all the same.

I sat down on the edge of the bed and ran my hand across his thin shoulder blades. I think I was needing to fix what was out of my control.

I pulled the gown closed across his back because everything else was unfixable.

He said, "I'm thinking I should miss the whole rest of this school year."

"I agree. Even if your vision comes back before then.

You have to take extra care of your eyes. With your temper, and the way you pick fights . . . I'm not sure I trust you to control yourself."

"I have to tell you something about that," he said.

He had metal cups taped over his eyes. Bandages underneath, then metal guards, vented to breathe, then tape to hold them in place. I could see the edge of one, just visible underneath the doughnut-shaped headrest.

"No you don't," I said. "You don't have to tell me anything you don't want."

We sat quietly for a moment, and I pulled the blanket up higher onto his back.

After a time I said, "Jake and Mona and I thought it might be a good idea if you did your recovery time at my house. Because I can work at home. I can work on my laptop by your bed and you'll have someone with you all the time."

"Jake and Mona went for that?"

"They think it's a good idea, yeah."

"I'm surprised."

"They love you," I said.

"They must," he said. "They really must."

On the day of his release, I helped Leonard into a cab in front of the hospital.

"What is this?" he said.

"What is what?"

"This. What am I getting into the back of? This is not your new car."

"No," I said. "It's not. It's a cab."

"Where's your new car?"

"It doesn't matter," I said. "It never did matter."

I gave the driver my address. Leonard sat with his face toward the window, as if he were looking out. As if he were able to see through the bandages and metal guards, and watch the familiar streets slip by.

"I'm sorry, Mitch," he said.

"Don't be."

"It was your new car."

"It was nothing," I said. "It didn't mean a fucking thing. I didn't even get it for myself. I got it to please Harry. Fuck Harry. Don't think another thing about it."

"Good thing we got rid of the cuss jar," he said.

## LEONARD, *age* 18: **ring around the moon**

I squat on the edge of this familiar cliff a moment longer, and look off into the night. I might never get to again. Maybe this look will have to last me. I think about what I'll miss if I leave. Like Mitch. Only I'd never really leave Mitch.

I made him a promise. I promised him for real.

I look out across the ocean.

There's a ring around the moon tonight. I've seen this before. Seen it and had it described to me, when I couldn't see it. I know what it really is. Ice crystals in the upper atmosphere. But I like to think it's something more. Like God underlining what's really important. Like Pearl with a halo. Like my new destination.

The ring around the moon I remember best was the one I never got to see. I was at Mitch's house, recovering from my eye surgery.

I'd gotten so housebound that I begged him to take me for a walk.

I remember his hands on my elbow, and I remember the puff of Moon Pie's breathing as he padded along behind. And I remember being scared.

I always thought I trusted Mitch. Completely. And I did trust him, but maybe not completely. More than I trusted anybody else, but not completely. When the chips were down, really down, I was surprised to find it was pretty much just Pearl and me.

"Trust me," he said.

"I do," I said.

But then I'd stop dead. Make a damn liar out of myself.

"There's nothing in front of you," he said.

So I'd take a step. But I kept picturing something in front of me. In front of my closed eyes I pictured an over-hanging tree limb. A flying object, like a bird or a thrown rock. And my eyes felt so vulnerable. So I'd stop in my tracks. Throw an arm up to protect them.

"Should we go home?" Mitch asked.

"No," I said. "No."

I hadn't been outdoors for so long. And it was only this trust thing threatening to push me back into bed again. I hated bed. I'd been there for weeks. So I let Mitch hold my elbow and I walked right through that imagined tree limb, and sure enough it wasn't there. Just like Mitch said it wouldn't be.

I felt myself strangely in his hands, and I realized I had

never been in anyone's hands before. Except with Pearl. By the time she died I was able to take care of my own fate and halfway save Mitch's ass in the bargain. I never really relied on him for much. I mean, material things, yes. I did. True. I'm not forgetting that he fed and clothed and supported me, and bought my glasses, and paid for my eye surgery with his brand-new car. It's just that in a deeper sense I felt I'd been on my own since age five.

I felt the air of that cool evening on my face, and I think it hit me then, for the first time, that the operation might not be a success. That I had better learn to trust Mitch if he said I was not about to slam into anything. Because this might not be a temporary situation. I could be taking his word for these things for the rest of my life.

It should have been a frightening thought, but I felt strangely settled. I felt a sense of peace, of knowing that I would live on and be all right either way.

We stopped in the little park near Mitch's house and sat down on a bench. Moon Pie came up in front of me and flipped my hand up into the air with his nose and I scratched behind his left ear. For some reason he likes to be scratched behind his left ear. Better than the right. Go figure.

"What's different about tonight?" I asked Mitch.

"What do you mean?"

"Just what I said. What's special tonight?"

"Nothing," he said. "It's just like every other night."

"No way. Wrong. No night is just like every other night. You're not looking close enough."

"I'm looking as best I can," he said. "Nothing's different."

"If I could see," I said, "I'd find something. You know I would."

"Yeah," Mitch said. "You probably would."

"So look the way I would. Come on, Mitch. It'll be good for you."

He was quiet for a full minute or two. Then he said, "There's a ring around the moon tonight."

"Good," I said. "That's a good start."

"What causes that?" he asked. "Do you know?"

"Ice crystals in the upper atmosphere."

"Oh."

Then we were quiet another couple of minutes, and I was still scratching behind Moon Pie's left ear. I stopped for a second, but then he bumped my hand to get me to start again.

Mitch said, "I think I did you a great disservice by not wanting to talk about Pearl. You needed to talk about it. I should have encouraged that."

"There was nothing to talk about," I said. "She died. It's not like I didn't know where she was or anything."

I could hear him take in breath. I felt the talk take a squirrelly, uncomfortable turn. A guarded turn. Like everything had all been just in its place until Mitch decided to shake it apart and make it go sideways.

"I know it's very hard to imagine that your mother could just leave you somewhere and disappear."

"It sure would be," I said. "Good thing I never had to think anything like that about Pearl."

"So maybe it's easier to believe that she died."

"She did die."

"We have no way of knowing that, Leonard."

"Sure we do," I said. "When a person starts showing up somewhere without her body, you can be pretty damn sure she died."

I think we talked some more about it, but it's hard to remember. I know Mitch talked more. It was like he had a dozen years' worth of stuff to get off his chest, and he seemed to be saying it just the way he had saved it up to say.

I wasn't sure how people did that. My thoughts changed all the time. I could never hold words in one place for so long.

Poor Mitch. What he thought Pearl had done was such a terrible thing. No wonder he was so worried.

I bet he didn't even believe that I could stay with him after I died.

I'm going to have to make a believer out of the poor guy.

I shudder slightly, not so much out of fear but out of excitement, wondering if this will be my moment. If this will be my chance.

I bring my attention back to the glider. And the cliff.

I untarp the glider, slip into the harness. Clip the harness in place.

Then I'm standing at the edge, in every possible sense of those words. Balancing the glider by the steering bar, feeling the wind lift it slightly. Already it feels like wings. Already it feels like *my* wings.

Moon Pie is bouncing around behind me, barking, the way he would if I were on the beach, about to walk into the surf. He can always sense when I'm about to go somewhere he can't follow. He hates moments like that.

I guess we all do.

I take three or four running steps. I don't jump, I just step. Then the ground falls away and I'm flying. Look at me, Moon Pie, I'm flying. Look at me, Mitch. No. Don't look at me. I forgot. This is something you wouldn't want to see.

I look down and see nothing but ocean. Black. I see the stream of moon reflected on the surface of the water, starting out at the horizon and pouring in like liquid light, like shiny liquid foil.

I feel the wind flapping in my shirt and rushing over my scalp and cooling my bare feet.

I look up and see that star. For some reason it looks brighter and shinier than any of the other stars. I feel like I can fly all the way out to it. Maybe even like it's asking me to.

So I turn away from the cliff, out to open ocean. And that's the direction I'm brave enough to fly.

The night we finally broke down and talked about Pearl was our night outdoors, after Leonard's surgery.

Up until then I'd been caring for Leonard in bed.

That evening I came in to find him sitting up on the edge of the bed, looking restless. His bandages had come off several days before. He could see shapes, light and shadow, but not much more.

"What are you doing up?" I asked. "Shouldn't you lie down?"

"Why?" he said. "Why should I lie down? I'm not sick. I'm in perfect health. I just can't see."

"I just thought you'd be more comfortable."

"Try lying in bed for a few weeks when you're perfectly healthy," he said. "And then tell me how you're most comfortable."

I sat down with him on the edge of the bed. "What can

I do for you, Leonard?" I asked, because clearly we had crossed a line, and my current level of care was no longer helping him enough.

"Take me for a walk," he said.

So I did.

It took a long time to get him to trust me. But then just when I thought he never would, he did, and I was taken with this strange sensation that Leonard was allowing me to guide him in a way he never had before.

It was a weird moment, and I'm not entirely sure how to describe it. I suppose it was a bit like suddenly being cured of a handicap you'd never realized you had. Because I'd never been anyone's parent before, and how was I to know how it was supposed to feel? And, not knowing how it felt, how was I to notice it was missing?

But that night, suddenly there it was. That sensation of being the leader. Being trusted.

I'd never consciously recognized it before, but always in the past, even at age five, Leonard either walked abreast of me or, all too often, took the lead.

I must have gotten too much of a sense of my own power, because I chose that moment to try to talk about Pearl.

Leonard slipped right back into the leading role, and in just a matter of a few minutes I was feeling stupid for not believing that she had died and was still hanging around somewhere.

Maybe I wanted to believe Leonard's version of events,

but it was hard. I guess I'm just not that much of an idealist. It's one of those things that sounds too good to be true. The love that can never be broken. The devotion that no power, no circumstance can pull apart.

The world was full of divorcing couples who swore they'd remain friends and now couldn't stand the sight of each other. The world was full of mothers who ditched their kids and ran.

That was the real world. Like it or not.

Leonard sat there quietly, listening to this interminable monologue on my part. All this stuff I'd been saving up for years. By that time it was all too rehearsed sounding. All full of guilt at having to teach reality. But he listened so patiently.

We were sitting on a park bench, and he was scratching behind Moon Pie's ear. Out of the corner of my eye I still saw that ghostly ring of light around the moon, and it made me sad that Leonard couldn't see it.

Ice crystals in the upper atmosphere. That's what he'd told me. And he was undoubtedly right. Why hadn't I known that? Why wasn't there anything I could teach him?

When I finally ran out of steam he said, "Poor Mitch. I'm so sorry you have to believe that."

That was it. The sum total of his reaction. Empathy toward me for not seeing the world his way.

And the really crazy part of the whole deal is that it wasn't just Leonard. Suddenly I felt sorry for me, too.

* * *

In the morning I got out of bed and made a strange decision. I decided that, at least for that one day, I would be blind.

I climbed down out of my loft and looked around for something I could use as a blindfold. I ended up with a clean dishcloth, folded lengthwise. I tied it around my eyes and then stood in the kitchen, wondering what I was supposed to do next.

Normally I would make coffee, read the paper, check my e-mail, and do the crossword puzzle. Already things seemed seriously off-kilter. It resembled that life shock of the type that sets in when there's been a major disaster. Nothing proceeds as usual. No routine goes unchanged.

I climbed upstairs and went back to bed.

After an hour or so, the lack of coffee began to seem like an issue. So I decided I would have to make some. Also, Leonard would wake up soon, and he would want some kind of breakfast. Cereal, at least. I would have to get myself to the kitchen.

But, you know, those damn ladder steps were a lot easier to go up than down. In my current nonseeing state, I mean. The fear of falling claimed every ounce of my attention. I should have learned years ago how many steps there were. I should have been able to do them in my sleep. But I fished with my foot for the floor, as if it might bite me when I found it, or as if I'd fall to my death if I didn't find it right there where I expected it.

When I got down onto the living room floor, I better understood Leonard's troubles of the night before. As I moved through the room, I kept picturing my face slamming into something. Even though logic told me there was nothing at that level. Still I walked with my hands in front of my face for protection. And promptly barked my shin on the coffee table.

Around the time I stubbed my toe on the kitchen doorway, I decided that shoes would be a good idea. So I climbed back upstairs, slipped on my leather Top-Siders, and had to do the treacherous downstairs climb all over again.

I did eventually make my way into the kitchen, but I felt as if I'd just survived a crawl through enemy territory during wartime.

I found the coffeemaker by feel, but I couldn't remember where I'd left the filters. Seemed I put them in a different drawer or cupboard every day. I would have had to look for them, which I could not at that moment do. I knew the box would feel like any other box. I knew they could be anywhere. I was quick to give up.

I found the paper towels on their rack over the sink. Something I kept in the same place every day. And I used one as a filter.

I always kept the coffee in the freezer. I found it easily, because it was in a distinctively shaped bag, but the freezer was crowded, and a shower of frozen foods rained down all around me, including onto the arch of my foot. I tried not to yell because Leonard was, I hoped, still asleep. I tried to gather up everything I had dropped, but I wasn't sure how far things might have rolled. Then I smacked my forehead on the kitchen table and decided to just make the damn coffee and let everything thaw on the floor.

Making the coffee actually went pretty well. I just used my hands to feel the fullness of things, the edges of them. I used my finger in the pot to judge when the water level was right, then I poured it into the coffeemaker with one hand marking the opening. I was beginning to feel proud of myself.

I opened the cupboard to get down a mug and knocked about half a dozen glasses and china cups onto the kitchen floor, where they shattered all around me.

I heard a slight sound, a rustle in the kitchen doorway.

"Mitch?" Leonard said. "What the hell are you doing in here? Repelling an alien invasion?"

"Don't come in," I said. "Don't come in if you're in your bare feet. There's broken glass."

"Duh," Leonard said. "I could have told you that from next door."

We both stood in silence for a moment, assessing each other in whatever ways are left over when two people experience familiar company in blindness.

"What are you doing, Mitch?" he said again, quietly, and I felt chastised. Caught at something wrong. Ashamed.

"Come here," Leonard said.

I crunched over some broken glass and kicked aside what felt like a can of frozen orange juice.

When I got to the doorway, Leonard reached his hands out and touched the dishcloth on my face.

"Oh, Mitch," he said and untied it in back, and pulled it away.

I blinked into the light. "I just wanted to see how hard things would be."

"Oh, Mitch," he said again. "Don't get me wrong, because you know I love you and all, but that's, like, the dumbest thing ever."

I felt stung, and I could hear it in my own voice as I defended my idea. "Why? Why is it dumb?"

"Because you have eyes. If you didn't, you'd cope with that. You'd manage. But you do. So don't waste them."

"I thought it would make me feel closer to you."

"When did we feel closest, Mitch?"

"I don't know. When did we?" I had thoughts on the matter, but this was my chance to hear his.

"How about last night, when we were out walking? Because you could see and I couldn't. We fit together because of that. There's nothing wrong with having something I don't."

"I just wanted to see the world through your eyes."

"Or lack of same," he said. "Voluntary blindness is never going to catch on. Believe me. Some things you don't do on purpose."

"Want some cereal?" I asked. Probably anxious to change the subject.

"Sure. Thanks."

"I'll bring it to you in bed. Let me just clean up this glass."

"With your eyes open," he said. "Or you'll cut yourself."

After he left I stood in the kitchen and looked around.

It was more like a dozen cups and glasses, actually. China mugs lay on their sides with the handles broken off. A tray of skinless, boneless chicken breasts sat half wedged under the stove, and two frozen cranberry juice cans had rolled under the kitchen table.

I poured coffee into the only mug left unscathed in the cupboard. Poured in a slug of half-and-half and watched the grounds swirl in the cup.

Then I set about cleaning up the mess.

About three o'clock that afternoon Cahill came by with his kid, John Jr. JohnBoy we called him. On their way to Little League.

I know it's hard to believe, but eight years earlier Cahill had gone and married Hannah.

I know. Believe me, I know.

First of all, Cahill was the guy voted least likely to settle down, have a kid, and drive him to Little League. Second of all, I'd always thought Hannah adored me. And maybe she did. I don't know anymore.

I just know that I liked to think of her as a sort of safety net. Which means I'd been working without a net for eight years.

Maybe it's not easy being somebody's safety net. Maybe she just didn't adore me enough. Maybe I'd treated her badly just by thinking she might.

Leonard was sitting cross-legged in a chair by the window. He looked like the Buddha or something. He also looked like he was looking out. Maybe he was. He could see some by then but we tried not to discuss how much. Too much pressure. Too hard to explain. He had a haze of beard growing, silky though it was, and I had been debating over helping him shave.

JohnBoy made a straight line, right through the living room to Leonard.

"Hi, Doc," he said as he breezed by, but it was clearly perfunctory. Leonard had all the pull. "Hi, Leonard."

JohnBoy thought the sun rose and set on Leonard. Of course I'm not claiming he was wrong.

"Hey, JohnBoy," Leonard said and reached out and ran a hand back and forth across John Jr.'s unruly hair.

"Can you see yet?"

"A little."

"How much?"

"Some but not all."

"What's it like?"

Leonard sighed. I knew it tired him to explain, but he didn't say so.

"It's like being in a dark room and just being able to see the very edges of things. Only it's not exactly dark. But that's about how much you get to see."

"Is it terrible?"

"No," he said.

"So it's okay?"

"Well. It's not something you'd choose for yourself." Then Leonard turned his face in my direction. Looked right at me, though I'm not sure how much he saw. Gave me a little wry smile. "Right, Mitch?"

"Oh, shut up, Leonard," I said.

When I woke up the following morning, Leonard was not in his bedroom. I looked for him everywhere. Even outside.

I asked Moon Pie's opinion. Out loud.

I said, "Moon Pie. Where did Leonard go?"

The dog was lying sprawled on the floor at the foot of my loft ladder. On the sound of Leonard's name, he looked up into the loft.

"Thank you," I said. "You're very helpful."

I climbed back upstairs to find Leonard asleep on the floor beside my bed.

He looked uncomfortable, so I lifted him and laid him

out on the bed. Amazingly, he drooped in my arms and did not wake up.

For three nights running, Leonard slept on the floor beside my bed, or on the couch at the end of the loft, or on the foot of the bed like a faithful dog. He never volunteered why, and I asked no questions.

On the fourth night Barb came to see me, and we had to slip downstairs to Leonard's room and make love on his floor with the door locked.

It was a hot summer night, and the only air-conditioning was upstairs in the loft. Leonard didn't mind the heat, but he hated artificially refrigerated air.

As Barb and I lay quietly together afterward, with me in that rare topside position, I realized that I had broken quite a sweat with my exertion. I felt a drop of perspiration roll off the end of my nose and watched it land on her collarbone in the half-darkness.

"He's admitting that he needs you," she said.

It was the first word spoken about Leonard, or anything else for that matter, since she'd arrived earlier that night.

It was out of left field, a continuation of nothing, a finish to a conversation never begun, and yet it fit right in, as if it had been expected, and I was not at all surprised to hear it.

"I know," I said.

"You should be flattered."

"I am," I said.

## LEONARD, age 18: don't you dare

At first I was cruising close to the edge of the cliff. Not all that high, either. Not that much higher than the cliff I launched from.

I knew I should nose up and try to get some altitude, but I just kept doing this. It was something like being a coward and taking too many risks, all at the same time. Flying close to the cliff made me feel like I could land any time. And I could. Potentially. It also made me feel like I could crash. And I could.

Then I saw it again, that one big star, right in front of me. Hanging over the ocean.

It might have been an illusion, but this is what I saw: There was a piece of light from that star, and it was reaching out to me. The wind made my eyes tear up, and the more I squinted through the tears the more the light from that star strobed out in my direction. Reaching for me.

And I felt like if I could just go a little bit faster, I could warp out to it somehow, and me and that light, we could meet in the middle somewhere, together. Don't know where, though. But Pearl would be there, even more than she is now, and it would be home.

I thought, what are you made of, Leonard? Whose son are you?

And I made a sharp turn out to sea.

The wind is strong in my eyes, I have those wind tears again, and I look at that star, waiting for it to reach for me again. Waiting for it to strobe out and take me home. But it's just sitting there, and the moon with the ring of light doesn't look like a destination anymore. It looks like a big stop sign.

And the ocean looks a long way down.

If that star is saying anything at all to me, it's nothing welcoming. If it's saying anything, it's saying, don't you dare.

Don't you dare throw your life away.

That's how I know I'm really close this time, and it jolts me. It jolts me hard and I get scared. I forget how much I've been wanting this and I start to feel like anybody else. Like I just want to live. That's all.

If Pearl is anywhere, she's in that star, or in the moon with the halo. Or more likely both. And she wants like hell for me to get back. And because I never knew that before, that's how I know I'm close this time.

It jolts me, and I turn hard. Way too hard. And I'm still

much closer to the cliff than I ever could have imagined. It felt like I'd been flying out to sea—toward that star—forever. But time played a little trick on me. The cliff is not that far away.

I dip down and head for the cliff but it's coming on too fast and I try to pull up but I pull way too hard and I stall. Because I was jolted. And I try to recover from the stall the way I learned but there's no room. It takes room to recover. And I don't have it. All I have is a big jut of cliff coming at me fast.

I know there's maybe something to do, but what is it?

There's no time to think.

The nose of the glider hits first, and hard. I want it to cushion me but it's too light and soft. I feel and hear the crunch of it, feel the aluminum pipes give way. The whole glider gives and bends and collapses and I swing forward in the harness and meet the cliff halfway and it smacks me in the head and the chest and the knee and then I'm falling. There's a spinning motion to the falling because the glider is so bent.

There are either rocks or ocean below, waiting to meet up with me, which is an ugly thing either way. So while I'm spinning it hits me—in that sudden abbreviated way that things hit when you wouldn't think there'd be time for any of that—what an ironic moment this is to realize that I want to live.

Rocks. It's rocks.

And a kind of shocked blackness that takes me away.

Sometime after I land—how long I don't know—I open my eyes and see the stars and the cliff up above me, blurred and muddied by the fact that I've knocked out my contacts.

Then my field of vision all goes black again.

And I think I'm blind. I think I've undone all Mitch did for me, torn my retinas or somehow knocked away all that good work and I'll never see again. I'm still trying to breathe. I think I broke some ribs and I know for damn sure I broke my leg and I still need to breathe. But it's all black with no air and then I go dizzy a moment and open my eyes and see muddy stars again.

And I realize I was passing out, not going blind, and I manage to pull in some air, but my ribs are cracked or broken and it hurts like hell.

But I'm alive, and I can see.

Moon Pie is on the cliff up above me. I can't see him, but I can hear him barking. Good boy, I think. Bark. Call attention. But it's one or two or three in the morning and I know there's nobody's attention to call.

So I lie on the rocks and breathe.

I have blood in my mouth. I touch the spot on my head. The spot I hit when I collided with the cliff edge. My hand comes away bloody. There's a lot of blood. I'm surprised how much. Then there's another place on the back of my head that I hit coming down on the rocks. My leg hurts so bad and I try to lift my head to look at it but something goes wrong.

Then I open my eyes, I don't know how much later, and I'm just seeing where I am again, and I remember wanting to look down at my leg, but I'm not sure what happened with that.

Moon Pie is still barking and I'm taking little shallow breaths because it hurts. I look up and Pearl is sitting on the rocks looking down at me.

I'm pretty sure, even now while it's happening, that she's not. Only she is. I mean, I really smacked my head. Pearl doesn't go places in her body, not anymore, but I smacked my head so hard and that's how I see her.

"Pearl," I say. "I missed you so much."

"Leonard," she says. "Don't get me wrong, because you know I love you and all. But that was really, really stupid."

She's just the age she was when I saw her last, about eighteen, and her hair is freshly combed, like a black waterfall. The wind is up on the ocean tonight and it blows hard across us, but her hair doesn't move. It doesn't blow. That's how I know she's not there, really. Except to the extent that she is.

"Why?" I say. "Why is it stupid?"

"Because you have a life," she says. "If you didn't, you'd deal with that. But you do. So don't waste it."

"I just wanted to be close to you," I say.

And then it hits me, in my delirium, that I'm repeating a conversation I had with Mitch when he tried to be blind for a day to feel closer to me. But I'm repeating it with the roles reversed.

"Voluntary death is never going to catch on," I say out loud. "It's just not something you'd choose for yourself."

*I* say that. So I'm saying both sides now. I'm saying the Pearl things, too. And then I open my eyes and Pearl is gone.

Or was never there.

I take little shallow breaths and lift my head to look down at my leg and it's crooked. I think I still hurt but it's getting harder to tell. I lay my head down again and close my eyes and I know things about myself I never knew before.

I know that I'm just a human guy, like everybody. I'm not some ethereal spirit who can magically transcend this life thing and go where I belong. I belong right here with all the other humans, and the only reason I ever thought otherwise is because Pearl is dead and I wanted her back.

The tide is coming in now.

A wave of it washes up onto the rocks and it's shockingly cold, like being thrown into ice water. It hurts my ribs and my leg and I yell out loud, and Moon Pie barks more desperately.

I have to find a way to crawl up the rocks and get out of this. Because it's cold.

But then a few waves later I realize it's worse than that. It's going to pick me up and dash me against the rocks and jostle my broken bones.

Just as I think that, it does.

It only moves me about one rock over and sets me

down. There's some pain, but now the coldness of the water is making me numb.

I don't realize the real potential of the situation until the biggest one yet washes over me, slaps me up against the face of the cliff, and then pulls me out to sea. I grab at rocks, but their faces are slippery and the pull is so strong. I try to swim, to fight against it, but my ribs are broken and I've hit my head so hard and the ocean is stronger.

I reach for what might be the last rock, but my hands slide away and I'm sucked out toward the sea.

And I think, that's it. I just found out how badly I want to live and now I've lost the battle.

My eyes break the surface, and I open them and see Pearl again. Sitting on the rocks at the water's edge. She doesn't look worried or upset. I'm about to raise my hand to wave good-bye when something stops me.

My harness.

The twisted, crashed glider has wedged itself firmly between two rocks. And I'm strapped to it, attached by this harness. The harness wins. The ocean loses. It pulls and pulls and recedes, and I wait for the glider to come loose, but it never does. It holds me. Then another big wave washes me up onto the rocks, jarring my broken bones. I try to grab for the glider, but I miss. And I have to do it all over again.

Again the glider holds.

Again I open my eyes and see Pearl sitting watching

me. And I realize that the tide is just beginning to come in. It's hours until morning. The battles I fought against these two waves will be a small part of a very long war. I realize if I want my life I'm going to have to put up a hell of a fight.

A wave crashes me against the rocks again. I grab an aluminum strut on the glider, wrap my arm around it, and hold on like I've never held on to anything before.

Pearl is still sitting—or not sitting as the case may be—just off my left elbow.

She says, "Do you think I wanted to die?"

"No," I say. "I think you wanted to stay with me."

"Damn right," she says. "I had no choice. You have a choice."

"I don't want to die either."

"Could've fooled me."

"I don't want to die now."

"Good," she says. " 'Bout time."

The waves are coming up higher now, and I'm so sure that each one is going to lift and unstick the glider and wash the wreck—and me—out to sea.

But I'm still holding on.

"You're my son," she says. "So you're strong."

I'm numb from the cold, and my whole body feels achy. I don't really want to talk, but it's Pearl, and she might not be around to talk to later. And besides, if I don't talk, I'll give up.

"Did you fight?" I ask.

Pearl says, "No."

"So why do I have to?"

"Because your dignity is not at stake," she says. "To keep your own life you give away anything in the world except your own dignity. That's the only thing you've got that's worth dying for. Now shut up and hold on," she says.

When I open my eyes again, she's gone.

I'm alone out here. I can't even hear Moon Pie barking.

I worry that I'm going to pass out and I'm worried about my sanity. Because of the way time stretches out. So I decide to sing. Or, I don't know, maybe I don't decide exactly. Maybe I just start. Funny thing is, I'm singing that song Pearl used to sing with me at bedtime. I wish Pearl was here to sing with me, but I can't honestly say I think she is.

Then after a while I just can't sing anymore.

I notice that I'm less in my body than I used to be. I can see me down there on the rocks, holding that glider. Not far down. But still. I worry what it means when I get outside of myself like that.

Then a few minutes or an hour later—I'm not able to figure time anymore—a big wave comes in and floats the glider and I can feel it lift up and I can hear the little scrape as it unsticks itself from between the rocks. Then the wave rushes out again and takes us. I'm back inside myself now. I'm hoping that's a good sign.

"I really tried," I say to Pearl in my head, but I know

she's not there anymore. Worse yet, I know she never was. I mean, not like that. I still believe I saw her in a candle flame and a sparrow but I don't believe she sat on the rocks and talked to me.

I feel like I'm tumbling under the surface of the water, bubbling along, and I can only hold my breath just so much longer. Then my face breaks the surface, and I'm out beyond the waves. And the war seems to be over. I've probably lost, but at least the war is over. It's strangely calm. Instead of the battering there's just a rocking swell.

I feel like I could pass out now and rest.

I can't decide if the glider will make me more likely to wash out to sea or to wash up onto the beach. But I figure I should decide soon, because I'm going to pass out. I have to take my best shot.

I unbuckle my harness. I've decided I'm going to try to swim to shore.

I don't feel cold now. I feel strangely warm and without pain. Very calm.

I take one good, brisk stroke, and I find the pain again. It capsizes me. Comes up through the numbness and I struggle and almost sink, and then I hold very still and wait for it to subside again.

I call out to Pearl one more time in my head.

I look at the moon and it all goes black and stays that way.

## MITCH, age 37: what grown-ups do

I arrive home from Jake and Mona's house thinking I shouldn't be here. I should be out looking for him. But I wouldn't know where to start.

We don't even know for a fact that he's out flying the glider. It's that obvious, awful fear, but we don't really know.

Let's say he took it out to fly it. He would take it pretty far away, I would think. How many hills are there in a fifty-mile radius of here? Part of me wants to visit each one personally. But probably I'll be of more practical use to everyone if I just stay by the phone.

I try to fit my key into the front door, but the door pushes open. Which is strange. I'm really pretty goddamn sure I locked it. I always lock it.

It opens with a slight creak and I step inside.

It occurs to me briefly—with a little jolt in my stomach

to go along—that someone could be in my house. But I brush the idea away again.

It's barely light. It's still so early in the morning that it's only about half-light.

I close the door behind me and look around. Sure enough, there's somebody here, sitting in the corner. It jolts me for a split second. But then I decide it looks like Harry. I decide it's probably only Harry.

"Harry?" I say. "Is that you?"

"Goddamn right it's me," he says.

The voice doesn't sound right. I mean, it *is* Harry. No doubt about that. But there's something in his voice that was never there before.

And there's something on the coffee table in front of him that was never there before. Something that doesn't belong to me. That coffee table was, miraculously, clean. I took everything off it so I could spread out some work night before last. Then I gathered up all the work and took it into the office.

I set Pearl's old envelope on the coffee table, next to whatever this is that Harry brought. I can see a big manila envelope, and it looks like a group of photos, eight-by-tens half spread out. Maybe black and white. But, photos of what—that I can't see.

I turn around to the lamp and switch it on to get some light on this situation, which is beginning to have a distinctly wrong feel to it.

When I turn back, all I see is Harry's fist. It fills up my

entire line of vision, flying directly at my face, and catches me squarely on the bridge of my nose.

The pain explodes like light and color behind my eyes, and then I'm sitting on the floor on my tailbone.

Man. Who would have guessed Harry could throw a punch like that one?

"You little prick," he says. "I gave you everything."

The pain in my nose is this amazing, radiating thing, like a cross between a sharp injury and the worst headache imaginable. The mother of all headaches. The original headache.

My hands are cupped under my nose. I want to bring my hands up to it, it's instinctive, but I can't bring myself to touch it. So they just freeze there under my face and it dawns on me gradually that they're filling up with blood.

I feel a wave of dizziness come around. When it passes, I crawl over to the couch and manage to hoist up onto it, and I lie on my back with my head draped back over the armrest. I'm hoping this will make the bleeding stop. I know I've gotten blood on everything. The floor, the Persian carpet, my jeans, the couch. It just seems like a thing to worry about some other time.

Meanwhile I'm not sure where Harry is, or what he's about to do next, or what to say to him. It seems I have to say something.

I want to say, Man, Harry, that's one mean son-of-a-bitch right cross you've got there. But it might sound flippant, and I think right now I'd better not be.

I say, "How'd you find out?"

But I say it quietly, and no one answers. I lie still and listen, wondering if he might have left. But then I hear him rustling around in the kitchen.

A minute later he comes back in with a plastic ziplock sandwich bag full of ice cubes. He sets this down on my face and I scream. Literally. Scream.

"I realize it stings," he says. "But it'll keep the swelling down."

"Stings hardly says it, Harry," I say when I can talk again. "Christ. I think you broke my fucking nose."

"Good," he says.

Then he sits down in the corner again. Picks up a drink which I realize he must have had by his side all along. The bottle is sitting next to the glass and it's mine. It's my Scotch from my cupboard, and since I rarely drink Scotch, it started out the night nearly full. But it's not nearly full now. And it dawns on me for the first time, in a clear mental picture, that Harry has been sitting here in my living room for some time, drinking my Scotch and waiting for me to get home so he could break my nose.

I decide not to even ask how he got in.

After a minute he reaches over and grabs up the photos from the coffee table—the ones I haven't seen yet—and throws them onto my legs.

I feel a wave of sickness as I pick them up, and I can't tell if its origin is in physical or emotional pain.

There are three of them. They're grainy black and

white, poor quality, and after looking at them for a few seconds I realize they were shot through my skylight. How, I don't know. Maybe from the tree or the telephone pole or the light pole up on the hill. I don't know what lengths someone might go to if a wealthy and influential man was willing to pay him to get photos.

What's really sad are the photos themselves. Because in them I'm not making love to her. I'm just sitting naked on the end of the bed watching her get dressed.

The only one I can clearly make out shows a kind of slump to my shoulders. She's putting on her bra and glancing over her shoulder at me like she just then remembered I was even back there.

It's like Harry paid some guy all this money to get photos of some hot affair, and what he really captured was this intense loneliness. This semierotic separation.

"You had her followed?"

"Yeah," he says. "I had her followed. To prove it wasn't you." Harry's voice has lost that tightness now. It sounds deeper than before. It sounds like he might be about to cry. "You think I'm stupid? I'm not stupid. I knew there was someone. I chose to let it run its course. Granted I didn't think it would take this long. I figured two years. Maybe four, tops. Marty kept trying to tell me it was you. I did this to prove how wrong he was. I said, Mitch is like a son to us. Of course he's close with her. He's like family."

In the following pause I can feel my nose throb. The ice is making it ache, so I lift it off, but that's much worse. It hurts much worse without it. So I set it back down with a little involuntary whimper.

"Why'd you do it to me?" he asks. "Were you jealous of my success? Is that it? Is it because I have more money than you do?"

I sigh. And wish we didn't have to do this.

I wonder where Barb is, and if she even knows that he knows. If she's off somewhere blissfully unaware that this is even happening.

"Money means more to you than it does to me, Harry."

"Well, you tell me, then. What did I ever do to you to make you want to do this to me?"

"I know this is kind of hard for you to fathom," I say. "But everything isn't always about you. I didn't do this *to you*."

"Bullshit," he says and takes another deep glug of my Scotch. I can hear him swallow. "Bullshit. Every time you fucked her you were sticking it to me. Be a man and admit it."

"I am a man," I say. "And I don't happen to see it that way. It was between her and me. We tried not to even let it get started. We tried not to even be alone together, only then it crossed that line and we couldn't uncross it again. I didn't know how to stop."

"You didn't want to stop."

"I couldn't stop."

"Bullshit. You can do anything you want. You didn't stop because you didn't want to."

I lie alone with that for a moment with my eyes closed. I guess it's not fair to say I couldn't have stopped it. I suppose I could have. It didn't feel that way at the time, but still. I was willing to stop it for Leonard. I let her walk out the door before I'd sell out Leonard. But for Harry I wasn't willing to stop.

"I ruined you today," Harry says. He doesn't sound pleased. He sounds almost regretful. "I put the word out that you and your little firm are not to be trusted. By close of business today you won't have one fucking client. You watch. You think they won't listen to me? You just watch."

He stands to go and I'm relieved. I want to call the office. See if the accounts really are flying away. I want to call Jake and Mona and see what they've heard about Leonard. I want to call Barb and see if she knows. If she's okay. If the bastard broke her nose, too, in which case I'll have to kill him.

"If you want," he says, "I'll drop you at the hospital. You can get that taped. Take a cab home. If you want."

"Pass. I have to stay by the phone."

"Your call, Devereaux."

He stops with his hand on the door. I wish he would just go. I will him to just go. But of course he has more to say. And it strikes me, as he opens his mouth, that maybe the least I can do is listen. That maybe I owe him that.

That I definitely owe him.

He wipes at his eyes with the sleeve of his sport coat. Like I won't know what that means. It's weird to think about Harry crying. Like a real guy or something. What if he's really been a real guy all this time with real feelings? Man, he must be hurting like all hell now.

Christ, look what I've done.

"Why don't you like me?" he says.

On any other day I'd blow this off, but this is not any other day. This is today, and I owe him.

"I guess I always found you a little . . . insincere."

Harry snorts laughter. "Oh, good," he says. "This is from the guy who comes into my home like family and takes all the business advantages I'd give my own son while at the same time he's fucking my wife for thirteen years behind my back. And he thinks *I'm* insincere. Let me tell you something, Devereaux. A little boy takes what he wants when he wants it. A grown man knows how much pain he's willing to cause for his own pleasure. It's a sign of maturity. Prioritizing somebody else's pain over your own satisfaction."

I decide to stand up.

I waver there a moment, steadying myself. And it works. I'm standing.

I look Harry in the eye, ice pack at my side, and I say, "I may not be the man you wanted me to be, Harry, but I *am* a man. Stop trying to take that away from me."

We lock into that stare for a moment, and then he breaks it first.

"If you try to see her again," he says, "I'll have both

your knees broken. Don't think I don't know where to get that done, because I do. It's over, as of yesterday. I just hope you get that."

Then he lets himself out.

I'm lying on the couch with my head dropped back, waiting for the phone to ring. I don't dare try to call the office, because Leonard might call, or Jake and Mona might call about Leonard, and then they wouldn't get through. I'm wondering how long I can go without having my nose taped. Wondering if I have aspirin, and if it's worth crossing the house for it, and if my queasy stomach could handle four or five.

What I never planned on was falling asleep. The funny thing is, I feel awake, but now I'm having this dream. That weird, vivid kind of dream you have in that half-asleep moment that really doesn't feel like sleeping.

I dream that I see Leonard on a busy street. He's walking quickly away. I have Pearl's envelope in my hand, and I want to get it to him, so I run to catch up. I have to push people out of the way. But Leonard is like a dream figure or a ghost. He keeps disappearing at the end of my hand. Turning up farther ahead. He keeps reinventing himself farther down the road.

When I finally catch up, I put one hand on his shoulder, and he turns around.

And it isn't Leonard at all. It's Pearl. She doesn't look very happy.

"I wanted to give this to Leonard," I say. "It's his birth certificate. I have to get this to him so he'll know who he is."

She shakes her head at me.

"Leonard knows who he is," she says.

The phone rings, and I jump. I scramble for it and pick it up, making my head hurt even more intensely.

"Leonard?" I say.

It's Cahill. "What the hell is going on down here, Doc? It's like a mass exodus. We've had five clients call in the last three hours to say they've suddenly decided to go with someone else. What do you know about this? What happened, Doc? What the bloody fucking hell gives?"

I hold my head for a moment.

Then I say, "I have to keep this line open."

"Fuck keeping the line open," Cahill says. "We've got fucking Armageddon going on down here."

"There's nothing I can do about it," I say. "There's nothing you can do about it. Just type up a résumé for yourself. See if you can't find some gainful employment. I have to keep the phone free for Leonard to call."

Then I hang up. I can still hear him ranting as the receiver touches down. A few minutes later, just as I'm getting settled back down, the phone rings again. And again I jump for it.

"Leonard?" I ask, more desperate than last time.

It's Barb.

"I know I shouldn't be calling," she says, "and I know this could get you hurt, but I had to see if you were okay. I'm sorry I didn't call sooner, before he got to you. But he just didn't take his eyes off me for a minute. If you know what I mean. Don't even ask me how he found out, because I have no idea. He might've had us followed. It didn't even seem like a wise idea to ask." A pause. I want to say that I never expected to hear from her again. But the words won't form. So the silence stretches out. "Is he gone? Are you there alone?"

"Yes."

"I'm coming over for just a minute. Just to see with my own eyes that you're okay. He'll be furious. But I'm going to tell him the truth, and I'll tell him it was my idea, and he can be furious with me. Okay?" Before I can answer, she says, "I just need to see you one last time."

I open my mouth to speak, but she's already hung up.

I sit for a while with the dial tone in my ear, the words "last time" ringing in my head. Not that I hadn't known in my gut it was over. Not that I even thought I'd be lucky enough to see her one last time.

Last time. One last time.

It's just something about the finality of those words.

I'm sitting up on the couch when she arrives. The door

isn't locked, and she lets herself in. I wish I'd taken a shower. I've been up all night and I'm exhausted and bloody and I don't feel clean. My hair feels dirty. My face is unshaven. I hate the sense of this as her last look at me. It isn't the way I wanted to be remembered.

"Oh, Mitchell," she says. "Oh, poor Mitchell. Look at you. Why didn't you fight him? Didn't you even try to defend yourself? My God, Mitchell, you're half his age. I can't believe you couldn't at least hold your own against him."

I'm so at a loss to answer that I don't even try.

I'm sitting with my eyes closed, and I feel her hand brush lightly through the front of my hair.

"You have blood in your hair," she says.

"I do?"

"Yes, right here." A brush of her hand again. "Dried blood."

"Oh." I wonder how I got blood in my hair. Since it doesn't tend to flow uphill. I decide it must have come from my nose while my head was dropped back.

"Come here," she says.

"Come here what? Come here and do what?"

"I'm going to wash your hair."

I follow her into the kitchen. Sit in a straight-backed chair at the kitchen sink, my head dropped back. She gives me a dish towel to put over my face, so my nose won't get wet. Though I'm not entirely sure why that matters.

I feel warm water running over my scalp, and then her

fingers in my hair. I try not to think of it as a potentially arousing experience.

"It just happened so fast," I say. "There really wasn't time to fight him." I have to move the towel slightly to get this out.

She washes my hair in silence for a moment or two. Then she says, "Is that it? Really? Or did you feel like you weren't entitled?"

"That is such a complex question," I say. "It gives me a headache just to think about it. Don't make me think about that, okay? I already have a headache without that."

"I just hate to see you get hurt," she says.

"Harry got hurt." I surprise myself, when I hear myself say it. "I hurt Harry plenty."

She never answers. She rinses my hair carefully. Squeezes out the excess water and towels it dry. Then she dampens a paper towel and gently cleans the dried blood off my face.

"That's better," she says. "I couldn't stand to see you with blood in your hair."

"So this is it? I mean, you're just leaving?" As soon as I say it, I feel a measure of her warmth slip away.

"What choice do I have?"

"You have choices. You have at least two choices I can think of."

"Please don't start with this, Mitchell," she says, in that voice that used to back me down. But she'll be out the door in a minute, for the last time. What's the use of backing down now?

It strikes me that the last time I made love to her will always be the last time I made love to her. That doesn't seem fair. I feel like I should have known that at the time. Maybe I could have appreciated it more. If I'd only known.

"Thirteen years," I say. "How can you just walk away from that?"

"I've been with him a lot longer than thirteen years," she says. Soberly. The way a stranger might talk to me. "And we have two children together. How can I just walk away from *that*?"

She's moving for the door now, leaving me sitting stupidly with a towel on my wet head. I stand and follow her to the door, knowing something desperately needs saying, knowing I better find it fast. Knowing I'm almost out of time.

"Did you love me?" I ask.

She stops in the middle of my living room. Stops walking. Stops everything. "What?"

"I think you heard me. I'm asking if you ever loved me." I wonder why I'm talking in the past tense. I guess it feels easier, less loaded that way, but I can't put my finger on why.

Then she does something strange. Or, anyway, it seems strange to me. She walks around behind me and picks up the towel, which I've dropped, and begins cleaning up the blood on the living room floor. But there's a dried edge to it that won't come up, and it seems to bother her.

She stops trying. Looks up and sees the blood on the couch. Everything is too much for her. Too much is out of order. I see her give up inside.

"Maybe club soda on that," she says.

And it strikes me how utterly ridiculous this is. I look at her and realize that she looks older now, and that I want to use that as an out but it isn't working. She still looks great to me. She'd still look great to anybody. But the really ridiculous part is that we're talking about club soda.

She stands up and drops the towel. "I was hoping that my actions would speak to that," she says. "I was hoping you might guess."

"It's not something anyone should ever be required to guess about," I say. "It helps to be told."

"It's hard for me to say things like that."

"I realize that."

"I'm sorry for the way things turned out, Mitchell. I'm really sorry about all this. I know you're hurting. But I don't know what you want from me."

"Forget it," I say. "Forget it. Never mind. Thanks for coming by. Thanks for checking in."

She walks out the door. For the last time ever.

It was over yesterday. I just didn't know it.

And now it's already today.

★ ★ ★

I swallow five aspirin all at once. Drink half a glass of water.

I look at myself in the mirror and it's worse than I thought. I have blood on my shirt and neck and hands, lots of it, and both my eyes are going purplish black.

I sit down on the couch and make a terrible mistake. I tempt fate by thinking I've just sunk as low as I can possibly go. I should have known better. For a split second I wasn't even thinking about Leonard.

A minute later there's a knock on the door.

I start to say "come in" but then I think better of it.

I walk unsteadily to the door. Look out through the peephole. Make sure it's not some large professional breaker of knees.

It's Jake.

My whole body, my brain, my bloodstream turn to ice. It's like a bad dream, a moment you've long anticipated, and all your mental preparation doesn't count for a thing when it finally knocks.

I open the door.

"Mitch," he says. He looks spooked. "What the hell happened to you?"

"Jake. Where's Leonard?"

"They found his glider," he says. "The glider got washed up on the beach."

"And . . ."

My ears are ringing waiting for the answer.

"We don't know," he says. "He wasn't with it."

## LEONARD, *age 18*: **love story with ocean**

For my fourth birthday, Pearl took me to the Santa Monica Pier. That way, she said, we could have an amusement park and my first look at the ocean, all in one day. Pearl took birthdays very seriously.

It was to be my day, all day, from sunrise to the time she sang me to sleep. A regular present can be unwrapped in just a minute, and then right away it can lose its shine. Pearl liked presents that just kept going.

"What's an ocean like?" I asked on the bus ride out.

"Sort of like a lake," she said. "Only much bigger."

"What's a lake like?"

"Sort of like Silver Lake, only nicer. No concrete and no fence."

"Because Silver Lake isn't really a lake, right?"

"Right."

"It's a resivore."

"Something like that, yeah."

"So what keeps people from falling right in?"

"What do you mean?" She was looking out the window. I think she was thinking about something else.

"If it doesn't have a fence like Silver Lake. What keeps people from falling in?"

"Well, it doesn't have slanty sides, the ocean. So you don't fall in. You have to walk in."

"Do people ever walk into the ocean?"

"Sure," she said. "All the time."

"Can I walk in?"

"Sure."

"Cool."

I walked in. And I think I screamed. I'm pretty sure I screamed. Because it was so cold and so wonderful.

I wanted her to pick me up so I could see where it ended. And she did. But of course I never saw where it ended. It was like infinity. I didn't know that word at the time. Infinity. But I knew that feeling. And later, when I learned the word, that feeling came back.

If Pearl had taken my hand and walked out into the ocean with me—just walked out forever, never to return—I would have followed her. I think I would have been relieved. Because I'd always had a desperate sense that Pearl was about to let go of my hand and walk off into infinity without me.

And, of course, I was right.

Maybe I knew.

Or maybe all kids think that. Maybe all kids have that fear and I was just unlucky enough to be right.

Anyway. It was an absolutely perfect day.

It was a rare time when we could spend the whole day doing nothing but loving each other. I spent the whole day being her son and she spent the whole day being my mother. It was my special day, so everything was just for me. I could not have been happier.

We drank orange soda and ate corn dogs and candy bars. We looked through the cracks in the boardwalk so we could see that the ocean was down there. And how far down it was. So we could get that crazy feeling, like falling.

I pulled the coating off my corn dog in chunks and threw it off the edge of the pier for the seagulls. Mostly the pieces floated down and hit the water and gulls would dive and scoop them up. But once or twice a gull actually caught one in the air. I couldn't believe it.

Hey. This is big stuff for a four-year-old.

We went on the bumper cars, and then Pearl let me play Skee-Ball. I think I was pretty good. Better than I'd expected I would be, anyway. I remember being pleased with how I did. And I know Pearl was good because she made the flashing "you win" lights come on once, and a ticket popped out of our machine.

That must have been how we got the giraffe.

Everybody we saw smiled and was nice to us. This guy we'd never even met drove us all the way back to Silver Lake, so we wouldn't have to ride the bus.

I miss her most when I think about that perfect day. She was happy then. We both were.

The part I remember best—because it was that memorable blend of terrifying and wonderful—was that time we spent under the pier. In the dark. I thought we were going to be down there all night, but I'm not really sure why. I can't remember if she'd said that to me or not. It was all so long ago. But for the night to catch us outside in the first place was quite an event. Pearl didn't believe in going out after dark. Especially not with me along.

Not safe.

So here we were doing something certified not safe.

It was great.

When you're a kid, and your parents don't keep you safe enough, all you want is to be safe. If you're overprotected, the way Pearl overprotected me, you want danger. Thrive on danger.

Or at least you're pretty sure you would. If you ever saw any.

So there we were under the pier, with the night all around us. Every time I took a breath, I could tell that was The Night coming into my lungs. I could hear the waves come in, a sort of hissing rush of sound. I could hear people clomping around over our heads, having fun, not realizing the sheer excitement of danger we all faced.

It's like the feeling I was searching for earlier that day, when I first saw the ocean. And I saw it as infinity, though I didn't have the word to put to it. And I wanted Pearl to hold my hand and take me there so I wouldn't be left here alone.

And now here we were in a night that was so risky and exciting it was like death. And I got to go there with her.

And then just that quickly she scooped me out of there and we were gone. On our way home.

And yet the whole day was perfect.

I was also partly relieved to go home.

Pearl got me two real presents while we were there. One of them I still have. She got me a stuffed giraffe. And she got me a strip of pictures of us together. I think she won the giraffe playing Skee-Ball. My memory is a little hazy about that. Because I remember some guy running after us and catching up with us in the merry-go-round place, and he had that stuffed giraffe with him. So I figured she won it and then forgot to take it along. It's the only explanation that makes any sense.

So when I woke the following morning my head was full of a day so perfect, so full of a world I'd never even seen before—never knew existed—that I felt it couldn't possibly have happened. It could only have been a vivid dream.

But then I woke up all wrapped around this stuffed giraffe that Pearl had won for me, and the pictures were on my pillow, waiting.

So it was one of those dreams that happened for real.

I still have the giraffe. Mitch went over to Mrs. Morales's house and got it for me, pretty early on. But Pearl had taken those pictures, at my request, and put them someplace safe. And I never knew where that was.

Twice when I got a little older I went over to Mrs. Morales's house and asked was there anything else Pearl had left behind. She said no, she'd boxed everything up and taken it to Mitch's house when she re-rented the apartment.

When you know you'll never see somebody again, and you lose the only remaining pictures, it feels huge. It feels like you've lost everything.

Maybe the pictures were with her. Maybe she had lost them, but I doubt it. Because she knew how important they were. Maybe I dreamed up the photos and they never existed. But I don't think so. I remember them pretty well.

So, now, when I finally see them again, this is how I know that I'm dead.

Because I have this dream where I open my eyes, and the first things I see are those pictures. I guess *dream* is the wrong word, but that's how it feels. They're on something like a metal bar, and I can vaguely see a white wall behind. Then I have to close my eyes again. Because there's pain.

So then I think maybe I'm not dead after all. Because if

I'm dead, there wouldn't be pain. Then again, if I'm alive, there wouldn't be those pictures. Because they're long gone.

It makes sense. It makes good sense to think that the other side is a place where you can open your eyes—figuratively speaking, of course—and see the one thing you lost that you want back the most.

Like when you play chess, and you get a pawn all the way to the far end of the board and you can ask to get a piece back. A fallen man, restored to the battlefield, just like that. So of course you take the most important one.

Maybe I'm alive and I'm dreaming.

I feel somebody take my hand, and I'm hoping it's Pearl, but I'm spinning back down now and there's just no way to tell for sure.

I try to open my eyes again, but they feel heavy, and there's pain, and I feel like I'm dipping down again, back into the dream.

And that's all I know for a really long time.

MITCH, *age* 37: **while leonard sleeps**

Jake and Mona come and go.

I stay.

Jake comes in the early mornings, before work. Before it's even light. Sits a minute and watches Leonard sleep. But there's a sense of helplessness in that. So then he goes to work. He comes back around dinnertime, usually with Mona, who has already come at least once, midday.

I'm here when they come, and when they go. Watching Leonard sleep. If that's the right thing to call it. Maybe he's in a coma, but I refuse to think in those terms. As far as I'm concerned, he's just healing. Resting until his battered body comes around. Which I'm convinced it will.

Besides, yesterday he opened his eyes.

His hospital bed has rails on each side, and they're raised, so he can't roll out. Why they think he might do that, I'm not sure. But I brought the pictures Mrs. Morales found in her wall, and I folded a little piece of tape on the back of them and stuck them lightly to one of the rails.

And then yesterday he opened his eyes.

I thought for a minute he was looking at me, but his eyes seemed unfocused, and then I realized he was looking at the pictures. Or, anyway, in their general direction. Whether he was able to know what he saw I can't say. Couldn't even guess. But some of it must at least have registered unconsciously. So maybe some part of him knows they are up here, waiting.

Which is the idea.

I'm bribing him to come back to me.

I grabbed his hand so he would know I was here but his eyes just closed again, and I haven't seen anything from him since.

This morning a doctor came in and taped my broken nose. Packed it, and set it with a small plastic brace, and taped it in place. It was beginning to hurt a little less. Now it's killing me again. But it was nice of him to do it, anyway.

The nurses tried to get me to leave Leonard's room to get it taped, but I wouldn't budge. So they worked it out another way.

Now I've got more of my own pain to deal with, and that makes it harder to just sit here and wait. So I wander down one floor to Pediatric Oncology and I borrow a couple of books. *The Cat in the Hat* and *Green Eggs and Ham*.

Not for me. For Leonard.

I bring them upstairs and I read them to him, over and over, my voice sounding weirdly nasal to me.

And I try not to cry, because the last thing I need is to have to blow my nose.

Leonard has two big gashes on his head, each with a nasty little track of stitches, each ringed with bruises and swollen out of shape. It's hard to look at. But I'm getting used to it by now. It's part of him. Part of the reality of his life right now, along with the taped ribs and the badly broken leg. It's the whole story, with nothing kept from me. No pleasant little lies. Like, I was the one that started those fights, Mitch. Life has just beat Leonard up bad, and it's all right there for me to see.

So I try to be big about it. And I read him *Green Eggs and Ham* again.

Then a nurse comes in and smiles, and I ask her if I can get some more books.

"What kind?" she wants to know. Like she hates to assume that I want kids' books.

"The type of thing you'd read to a five-year-old," I say. And then after she's left the room I say, "Who's just lost his mother."

A few minutes later she brings me some things I might not have picked out on my own, but they're fine. One about a troll under a bridge and one about a big clumsy puppy who means well but causes trouble.

I wish I could remember that song Leonard used to

sing when he was trying to get himself to sleep. That would be perfect right now. But it's a hard thing to remember because it didn't have any real English words in it. It didn't make any particular sense.

It's getting harder not to cry.

Sometime in the middle of the night I think I hear his voice, and it wakes me. I'm sleeping in a cot beside his bed, and I think I'm dreaming.

"Mitch," he says. "Hey." His voice sounds whispery and weak.

I turn on the light but his eyes are closed, so I think again that I dreamed it.

"Mitch," he says again. This time I see his lips move.

"Yeah, Leonard," I say and take hold of his hand. "Yeah, I'm right here." I wish he would open his eyes and look at me but he never does.

"If you died, and you could stay around as long as you wanted and take care of somebody, who would you stay for, me or Barb?"

He's slurring his words like a drunk.

The use of her name slices through my gut like blunt, rusty metal. I've been trying not to think about that.

"You," I say. "Definitely you."

Leonard smiles the slightest bit. Which is just the most wonderful thing to see. "You're really getting this forever love thing, huh?" At least, I think that's what he said. He's not forming the words clearly.

"Yeah," I say. "I think I'm finally paying attention about that."

I sit up all night waiting for him to say more. He never does. I sit with him all morning thinking this will be the morning he wakes up. It's not.

Later that night, just as I think I'm about to go to sleep, I open my eyes. Leonard's face is turned slightly in my direction on his pillow. My eyes are fairly well adjusted to the dark. And it looks like his are open. It's like he was staring at me, and I felt it, so I opened my eyes.

I turn on the little reading lamp beside the bed and he squints and makes a disapproving noise.

"Sorry," I say. "You're awake."

"I think I was dead," he says. He still sounds a little drunk, but less so. He's on a morphine drip, so I guess it's reasonable for him to be less than sharp. But he sounds like he's fighting it. Trying to be present.

"When?" I ask. "For how long? Because, you know, you're definitely alive now."

"Yeah," he says. "I know. I hurt like hell."

But then I get a sense that he's tired, that it was a lot of work just to say that much. So I don't push him to tell me when he thinks he was dead. He just lies there with his eyes flickering open, and then closing again. Then opening. Then fluttering closed.

A few minutes later he looks at me and says, "You look awful. What happened to you?"

I smile and say, "Tell you some other time."

"You look worse than I feel."

I notice that the photos of Leonard and Pearl have gotten knocked down, so I pick them up and stick them onto the railing of his bed again. His eyes flutter open, fix on the photos, and stay that way.

"Mitch," he says. It's a whisper. "Is that really there? How did that get there?"

"I put it there for you to see."

"Where'd you get that, Mitch?"

"Mrs. Morales found it in the wall. The night before your accident. She gave it to me about a minute before you turned eighteen. It's almost like a birthday present from Pearl."

That and a last name, which I'll tell him about as soon as I'm sure he's with me enough to register. To remember.

He blinks for a minute. I get the sense that he's resting up to speak. I remind myself I should be elated that he's awake and talking but, truthfully, I never doubted it. I never thought it would be any other way but this. I wasn't going to settle for any less. I wasn't about to lose everything. Everything else, that's fine. But not Leonard.

"Well. Pearl took birthdays pretty seriously," he says.

Then a strange noise comes out of him, small and

265

whimpery, and I think he must be in a great deal of pain. Some kind of rough spasm brought on by pain.

I'm reaching to ring for the nurse when I realize he's crying.

So I just sit quietly with him instead.

I want to hold him but I don't dare. I can't think of any good, uninjured place to grasp him by. So I just take one of his hands and sit with him while he cries. After a while I get up and bring a box of tissues. Wipe his nose like he was a five-year-old.

This is the activity that takes up most of our first night.

I'm not surprised. I've been expecting this. Sooner or later he was going to break down and mourn the loss of his missing mother.

I just never thought he'd be eighteen years old at the time.

When I finally get to take Leonard home—I'm pleased to say I can honestly call this his home again—he's still in a wheelchair. Improving, but not ready to haul that cast around on crutches. Not with a slightly impaired sense of balance and all those broken ribs.

He sits patiently in the middle of the living room while I bring in the mail. I haven't been home for days.

"Do I get my old room back?" he asks.

"Yeah, I cleaned it out for you. Brought a lot of your

stuff from . . . Jake and Mona's." I almost said from home, but I have to remind myself. This is home.

"Check your messages," he says. "Your message light is blinking. Didn't you even go home to check your messages?"

"Not really," I say.

"Feed those poor birds. Oh, poor Pebbles. Poor Zonker. Do they even have water?"

I check, and they do. But it's low, and it's filthy, so I replace it. I hate to admit I'd forgotten all about them. I bring them two scoops of the big bird mix, with dried red peppers and whole peanuts and almonds in the shell. And I put a whole apple in there for Pebbles to work on. She takes that opportunity to try to bite me for what I've done.

"What if they'd needed you at the office?" Leonard says.

"There is no office."

"I have no idea what you're talking about, Mitch."

"There's no more business. It's gone. Evaporated."

"Just like that?"

"Just like that." I walk over and hit the play button on the machine. Sort through the mail while I listen.

The first message I've already heard. But, after hearing it, I didn't hang around to erase it. It's Mona.

"Mitch," she says, her voice already a desperate tumble. "We found him. He's alive. He's in the hospital in really bad shape but he's alive. He was drifting over by the boat

CATHERINE RYAN HYDE

launch and some guy saw the glider when he put out fishing this morning. Before it even got light. It's like a miracle, Mitch. He'd managed to pull himself up onto the glider just enough that it kept him floating. And the glider didn't sink, even though it was all twisted up. You gotta get down here, Mitch. He's been at the hospital for hours. Long before the glider washed up. But they didn't know who he—"

Mona keeps talking, but Leonard interrupts. Talks over her. "That's kind of weird," he says.

"Which part?"

"I really don't remember pulling myself up onto that glider. I'm almost sure I was in the water when I passed out."

"Maybe you pulled yourself onto it *after* you passed out."

I'm kidding, but not completely. Sometimes you do weird things when you need to badly enough. Things you never thought you could do, that are supposed to be impossible. Pick up a car. That sort of thing.

The message changes. We hear the click of a new message and we stay silent and we wait. First there's nothing. No voice. Like it's going to be a hang-up.

Then three words. Just three. In a voice so familiar I could cry.

"I loved you."

It makes my scalp tingle in a weird way and I decide it would be a good idea to go sit down on the couch, so I do.

Leonard says, "That sounded like Barb."

"It was."

"Why was she saying it in the past tense like that?"

I breathe deeply. As deeply as I can around this big boulder in my chest.

I've been so focused on Leonard, and that's been very convenient. A way to cover another crushing loss, but it's still out there, I know. Waiting for its moment. Waiting to come inside. To insist it be felt.

Like now.

"Thing is," I say, "that sort of evaporated, too."

"Just like that?" he asks.

He looks small in his wheelchair in the center of the room. His huge leg cast is propped straight out. His hair has begun to grow back around the head wounds. Now that he's sad for me, he looks smaller and more wounded.

"Just like that."

"Poor Mitch," he says. "After all those years." Then we sit quietly for a moment and he says, "Even so, though. I don't see why the past tense. I mean, she didn't stop loving you just in the past few days. Did she?"

"I don't suppose so," I say. "I think it's just a shield she uses. To be able to say a thing like that at all."

Leonard nods. I can see him fitting this together in his head, meshing it in with a lot of other information he's seen with his own eyes and knows to be true.

"Poor Mitch. You really lost everything, huh?"

"No," I say. "Not everything."

269

CATHERINE RYAN HYDE

I wheel him into his room and help him over onto his new bed. It's hard, because if I hold him tightly I'll hurt his ribs. And if I don't he might fall.

I do the best I can, and he barely makes a noise, but I can tell it's not a pleasant moment for him.

"It's weird," he says. "I really don't remember pulling myself onto that glider. I was pretty sure I was in the water when I passed out."

"You must have really wanted to survive."

"I did," he says.

"Obviously," I say.

270

## LEONARD, *age* 18: **love in the present tense**

Why do I feel so young right now? I really haven't figured that out. I don't even think I'm trying. More giving in to it. Letting it have its way.

It's about midnight, but I'm not asleep. Of course, I've been sleeping all kinds of crazy hours. Like all day.

But now it's night, and it's dark. And I'm alone. And it makes me just a little bit lonely and scared.

"Mitch?" I call it out pretty loud. His room is right upstairs from mine. If I could just reach that high I'd knock on the ceiling. Because it's important. "Mitch?" It hurts my ribs to yell. But I still do.

It's amazing how much this already feels like home again.

A minute later he comes stumbling in, looking at his watch. It's not on his wrist. He's just holding it in his hand when he comes through the door. Looking at it. There's just enough light for me to see him doing that. Not enough for him to see what time it is.

"I think it might be too early," he says.

Which seems a little bit confusing. Because if anything I'm calling for him too late at night.

"Too early for what, Mitch?"

"Your pain medication."

"That wasn't it."

"Oh. What?"

He sits on the edge of my bed with me. And then I feel sheepish and strange.

"I don't want to sleep alone. Can I sleep in your room like I used to sometimes?"

I hear him breathe in the dark, and then he says, "I don't know how we'd ever get you up to the loft."

"We could do that piggyback thing. Where I hang around your neck."

"Leonard. That was a really swell trick when you were five. Right now I'd worry about dropping you. What if I brought the rollaway bed in here and slept right here in your room?"

"Okay," I say. "That would be good."

After he's all moved in, just before he settles in to sleep, I say, "Light a candle. Okay, Mitch?"

I'm hoping he's awake by now so that we can talk for a while. I really don't feel like going to sleep.

He has to bring a candle down from the loft.

Then, when he lights it, I realize that I'm about to get the answer to a significant question. And I feel scared, like I'm not ready to know yet. So I keep my eyes squeezed tightly shut.

I'm lying on my back facing the ceiling, watching the flickery glow against my closed eyelids.

"You know what else is weird," I say. Like we never stopped having that old conversation in all these hours since we last talked. "I keep looking at those pictures of me and Pearl. And she looks so worried. We were having this wonderful day that was nothing but fun. But she looks all distracted and scared. And now I don't know why."

"She was a grown-up," Mitch says. "An extremely young one, but still. Grown-ups always have some unfortunate thing on their minds. Why are your eyes all squeezed shut? Are you okay?"

"Tell you later," I say. "Tell you when you tell me what happened to your face."

"Ah," Mitch says. He doesn't sound sleepy. "I see. Are we moving into one of those new phases where we tell each other the God's honest truth?"

"Maybe so," I say. "I think so."

"Okay. I guess I can deal with that. Harry broke my nose."

"Oh."

"Because he found out about me and Barb."

"Oh." I sit on that for a while and then say, "Who

would have thought Harry was capable of all that passion?"

"That's what I thought," he says. He sounds excited to have his thinking seconded like that.

It feels good that we're talking. Really talking. About things that matter. About things that are true, even if they don't show us in the most flattering possible light.

My eyes are still shut tight.

I say, "He must've been crushed."

"Yeah," Mitch says. "I really hurt the guy."

"So we're both feeling pretty guilty right now." He doesn't even ask. Just waits patiently. Gives me time to gear up to elaborate. "I know I've put you through a lot, you and Jake and Mona and the other kids. All the people who love me. I know this has been really hard on you. I'm sorry for being so stupid."

"Apology accepted," he says, and we lie quietly for a long time.

I still haven't opened my eyes.

Then Mitch says, "Can I ask you a really important question?"

I think I know what he's going to ask. Even though it's a mile from anything we've just been talking about.

"You want to know if Pearl is still with me."

"How did you know I was going to ask that?"

"I don't know. I just knew."

"So. Can I ask?"

"I'm not sure."

"You're not sure if I can ask?"

"No. You can ask. I'm not sure if she's still with me. I'll tell you in a minute."

I open my eyes. I look at the candle flame and know. It's a sweet, good-feeling kind of knowing, even though it isn't quite the answer I want. The flame has this openness to it, like it still contains a sacred space, but right at the moment it isn't occupied by any sacred person, place, or thing in particular.

"No," I say. "She's not still with me."

"Oh."

"But thank you for believing that she was."

"Anytime, Leonard."

"You know what this means, don't you?"

"No. What does it mean?"

"It means I'm going to be okay. Because no way would Pearl move on unless she knew for sure I was going to be okay."

"Agreed," Mitch says.

Then we're quiet for so long that I think he's fallen asleep.

Just so I'll know for sure if we're done talking, I say, "Mitch. I love you."

"I know," he says. "I love you, too, Leonard."

"Right now," I say. "In the present tense."

"I knew that's what you meant. That's the only kind of love you do. That's why we keep you around."

"Oh, is that why you keep me around."

"That and the cool tattoo," Mitch says.

First off, I just want to say it's weird to write a letter when you hardly even know to who. I mean, you can't even say, "Dear so and so," like you would normally do. You can't even figure out how to start. But I guess I started, anyway, so here goes.

The other thing is weird—in my head I see you as being about four or five years old, because the only time I ever saw you, that's what you were. I know you're a grown man now, probably thirty or close to it, but I still close my eyes and see that kid with the hair that stuck up. Since that's all I know of you, all I saw with my own two eyes. I just saw you that one time.

I know I'm doing a terrible job of this and I'm sorry.

What I want to say is that I know what happened to your mother that night, and you got a right to know, and should have, long before this, and for that I'll always be sorry. At least, as long as I live, so I better be sorry pretty fast, but I'll get into that more as I go on.

Another weird thing is to be writing so much from the heart to someone who probably won't ever get this. Also knowing you'll hate me if you do. But probably you won't even get it. I'm going to give it to my daughter and have her take it by that house where you and your mom used to rent a room. Maybe that lady will remember. Seems to me when somebody rents a room to a young girl who disappears without a trace one day (leaving her kid behind) that would leave an impression and probably you wouldn't forget.

I've never forgotten where the house is, because I went by there four or five times that first year. Once I sat outside for almost an hour, smoking cigarettes and wondering should I just go inside and tell the truth. But I guess you can see how it worked out. I guess it wasn't right when I said I saw you only that one night. I saw you through the window of the house next door. A couple weeks later I guess. You were sitting on the couch watching TV with that guy who lived there. I wonder if he still does. Maybe my daughter should give this letter to him. Unless he's moved on. It was such a long time ago. Twenty-five years by now. But I remember, though. You had thick glasses and your face was so small it just broke my heart.

I got kids of my own. Just so you know. They're all grown now, like you. I just wanted you to know.

Brace yourself for what I'm about to say. You probably

know it already, in some part of you, but it's different when you hear it straight out, like a fact.

Your mother died that night.

I didn't kill her, but I didn't stop it happening either, which I know I should have done. Actually, I tried. More than once I tried. But as soon as it was the next morning and the sun was up and life was supposed to go on from there, I could see real plainly that I didn't try nearly hard enough.

I just can't tell you how sorry I am.

I know the question you must have on your mind now, and I don't blame you. Of course you want to know why, and I don't blame you one bit for needing to.

I don't really want to tell you because I don't want it to seem like I'm talking bad about your mom, but you deserve to know.

My partner knew for a fact that she killed a very, very close friend of his a few years earlier. His partner, which is a very sacred thing, which I don't expect you to understand. Benny was not a bad man. I know that's a hard one for you to swallow, but it's true. He was an angry guy and he did a lot of things wrong but always on the way to trying to do them right. And we went out there that night thinking no one would get hurt.

Can you understand what I just said? Most people probably wouldn't, especially with their own mother. Hell, if it was my mother I'd kill him, no matter what he meant by it.

But you can't kill Benny, because it's way too late for that. He took care of that for you, years ago. I won't say it was all about what happened with your mom, because Benny had lots of problems, but that sure didn't help. Guilt does funny things to a person. See this is why you should be careful of the things you do. Because if you do something you know in your gut isn't right, you'll start to feel like you don't deserve good things. Like you don't deserve anything. You don't do right for other people, you do it for yourself. Can you understand what I just said with that?

Not that you need a lesson in living from me. Not that I got a right to tell anybody else what a right life is. Only, sometimes you can learn what not to do, and that helps. I could give you a lot of life directions in what not to do.

There's a reason things got out of hand, and it's a little delicate, so please try to hear this and take it the right way. It seems that her relationship with this guy who got killed (Benny's partner who I mentioned before) was personal in nature. And since she was a young girl and Len (that was Benny's partner who got killed) was married and had a couple kids, Benny thought it was important to Len's family that this delicate part of what had happened not come out. So he was just trying to get her to change the story.

I think now that he was wrong about that, that people need to hear the truth whether it'll feel good to hear it or not, because it's still the truth. Which is why I'm writing this to you now. But Benny believed that with all his heart, and thought he was doing the best thing out of a lot of possible bad things (if that makes sense). Not that he thought it was right exactly, more that he thought everything else was even worse wrong. Benny was really big on justice, and sometimes a guy like that can do a lot of harm, because justice isn't really our job (if you know what I mean). But I gotta say again that what he intended was just to change her story. He was not a monster. He was not an awful man.

I kept my mouth shut so I wouldn't be turning him in. But it wore on me. I mean that for a fact.

I know you're probably thinking, okay, but what about when Benny died? I thought about it. I thought about coming clean, even though I knew I'd lose my job and go to jail. But I didn't, and I'll tell you why not. Because I got a wife and four kids, and my kids were just going into college and my family needed me, and it was not their fault. They were the real innocents in all this, them and you. I couldn't see getting it off my chest to bring relief to myself when they were the ones that would suffer the most. It didn't seem right.

I guess you wonder why I'm coming clean now.

Well, it's pretty easy to explain. About four years ago I got lung cancer. I had surgery, and so much chemotherapy I thought it would kill me, but it looked real good. Doctor thought maybe we pulled it off. But now it's back and it's everywhere, in my belly, in my bones, even in my lymph glands. Now the doctor doesn't have much to say.

All he says to me now is, "Get your affairs in order, Chet."

I never exactly knew what that meant. What affairs, and what order are they supposed to be in?

I finally just asked him. He said it means that you have to do up anything you left undone, like tell your wife you love her and tell people stuff you should have told them a long time ago, but you've been putting it off. Because you can't put it off much longer. You know who the first person was I thought of? You. Really, you. I'll have to tell my wife I love her and tell my kids I'm proud of them (all except the one but I will think of something nice to say to him anyway) but the first person I knew I had to get my affairs in order with was you.

I really hope I can get this to you somehow.

I'm putting my return address on the envelope, and if you get this in time, if you want, you can come see me.

I know you'll have a lot of rage, and if you want to come over and take it out on me, that's okay. I'm a dying man and I'm in bed and can't fight you back, but, seriously, if you want to come beat the crap out of me you can. I owe you that much.

I can't give back what I took from you and no amount of "I'm sorry" will mean much but if you want to do something to me to get all that anger out of your system I can let you do that, and maybe that's something.

Even if you want to strangle me. I hope you don't of

course but if you do I deserve it and I guess I was going soon enough anyway.

What else can I say to you? I really wish I knew.

I'm sorry for my part in what happened.

Yours sincerely,
Chet Milburne

## LEONARD, *age 30*: **look over your shoulder**

It's funny, the things you think about. The things that come into your head. Like for example, while I'm driving to Southern California, to this guy's house, I'm thinking about the bogeyman. How I always thought I'd missed my chance to see him, because I didn't look over my shoulder that night Pearl went away. And I wonder, am I really going over there to ask questions, or do I just want to get a look at him now?

The first thing I see is his daughter. She opens the door when I knock. She's a big woman, and she stands blocking the doorway. Stands with her legs splayed apart and her arms crossed over her chest like some vertical pit bull. I've never met her. She gave the letter to Mitch and he gave it to me. But she seems to know who I am. She seems to have been expecting me.

"Not if you're going to hurt him," she says.

"I'm not," I say.

I don't expect her to believe me, but then I see that she does. Kind of gradually, but she does. She's looking at my face, and her own face is changing. Slowly, but still changing. So I guess I must have everything in the world on my own face except murder and abuse, which I'm glad to know. At least I'm coming into this the right way.

She stands aside and lets me by.

She follows me to his bedroom, calling directions as we go. The house seems dark and still, as if no one alive lives here at all, not even her. I wonder if she's dying as a way of being sympathetic.

I step into the bedroom and he's there in the bed. One of the men who killed my mother. After all these years, I'm standing in his bedroom taking a good look. His eyes are closed, so I can just look. No other drama for the moment.

All that emotion from all these twenty-five years wells up and races out in his direction, all the anger and the resentment and something that's one or two steps short of hate, but it's too close for my comfort all the same. And then all that emotion falls at his bedside and sits there on the floor looking foolish. Because he's just an old man.

He's terribly thin, arms just bones with skin stretched across, face transparent with dark bags under his eyes. Hair no color at all. The whole man no color at all, as if the color died first, leaving only the body itself to follow.

I wonder what I could possibly have done to this guy,

anyway, that would even come close to what he's doing to himself. I think, crime has so many victims. One single crime, against one single person. So many victims.

He opens his eyes. Looks at me like I'm here every day, every time he opens his eyes. "Dora, leave us," he says.

I expect her to argue but she doesn't. Maybe she argues with everybody else. But when her father says leave us she just fades away. And I'm alone with my bogeyman.

I pull a narrow chair up to the side of his bed and sit down.

He says, "Just warn me what you're going to do, okay? So I can brace for it."

"Nothing," I say. "Just ask you two questions."

We're both still for a moment while he takes that in. Then he reaches for a cigarette from the bedside table. It seems amazing to me. Some people start killing themselves and just don't know when to stop.

"If you don't mind," I say, "please wait until I'm gone. I won't be here long."

He brings his hand back down to his side again. Slightly uneasy. "Okay. Shoot with the questions."

"Tell me about Len."

"What about him?"

"Len—is that short for Leonard?"

"Yeah, sure. Leonard. Leonard DiMitri was his name. Why?"

The news spreads through my body like heat, starting in my belly and swimming through my bloodstream. I feel like I can't talk until it reaches my toes, or maybe I can't ever talk again. It's what I felt when I read the letter and found out Pearl was dead. Which I knew. I knew this, too. But I guess there's more than one kind of knowing.

"My name is Leonard," I say, when I'm ready to say something.

"Oh, yeah? That's a coincidence."

"Maybe." He doesn't seem to take that in or comment. I realize there's very little emotion in the room with us, between us. If any. Maybe he doesn't have any left. Me, well. I'm not sure what the explanation is for me. "Where can I get a picture of this Leonard DiMitri?"

"In the top drawer of my desk over there in the corner."

He points and I look over my shoulder, not quite prepared to believe it will be that easy.

"You kept a picture of him all these years?"

"Not exactly. It was in with Benny's stuff, and his wife was gonna throw it out when he died. There was all this stuff she was just taking to the trash. Didn't mean anything to her, you know? Doesn't mean all that much to me, either, but it was the most important stuff in the world to Benny, so I rescued it."

I stand up, feeling disconnected from my body. Feeling like I'm in a dream or a movie or something else besides my life, which seems to be all I can feel just now. I go over to the desk in the corner and open the top drawer. There's a policeman's shield and a couple of fishing lures or flies or whatever you call them, and a sportsman's knife of some sort, and a photo of Leonard DiMitri. I know it's him because he's in a policeman's uniform, full dress blues, and he's wearing a name tag. And I recognize him, in that funny half recognition you sometimes get with a face you've never seen before. Because the parts I recognize are me. Granted, we also look a lot different. Of course we do. He's a white guy and I'm as much Asian and black as I am white, but looks go deeper than that. People go deeper than that. There's the jawline, and the brow. And something around the mouth.

I pick it up. And I know I'm not giving it back.

"I need this," I say. "I need to keep this."

"Sure, whatever," Chet says. "My daughter'll just throw it out when I'm gone."

I sit down by his bed again, noticing that my hands are shaking just the tiniest bit. I just keep looking at the photo. Neither one of us says anything for what seems like a long time.

Then I say, "If Pearl did what you say she did . . . If she killed—" I almost said "my father." I almost said "If she killed my father." And I don't want to say that. It feels like a confidence, a private thing. Something I don't want this dying man to know about me. Something I'm not ready to share with anybody, so especially not with Chet. "If she killed the man in this picture, she had a reason why she did what she did. I'm not saying she was justified, that killing's ever justified. Just that if you could go back and get inside her head and know everything, then you'd know why. Because I know there must have been a why. Because Pearl wouldn't do a thing like that for no reason. Do you understand what I'm saying to you?"

I look up from the photo, into Chet's eyes. For the first time, I see emotion there. A positive emotion, like he's leaning in to me. Striving for some kind of closeness.

"Of course I do," he says.

"You do?" Once again something feels like it's happened too easily.

"Sure. What do you think I was trying to explain to you about Benny?"

My brain shuts down and I decide I can't think about these things anymore, at least not now. I'm tired from this.

"Where is she?" I ask.

"Who?"

"My mother."

"I thought we were clear on that."

"I'm talking about her . . . remains. Where are they?"

"Oh," he says. "That. Out in the middle of nowhere. Halfway to hell and gone."

"So you don't know? Or you won't say?"

"I don't know that I can even remember. It was a long time ago."

"You didn't go by there four or five times that year like you did with my house?"

"No. No, not there. Didn't wanta go back there."

We fall quiet, and I feel a trace of anger forming. Because I wanted two things from him and he only gave me one. I think it's been waiting, wanting to form. But then he dropped this picture in my hand and changed the subject. But now, with that anger, I feel better.

Chet breaks the still. "I was sitting in the car that night for what felt like forever. Looking around. I can still see the spot like it was yesterday. I can see the angle of the power lines, and the way the road curved. But I could never tell you how to get there. I know what route we took to go up into the mountains. But I don't know the name of it. I just know the spot where we turned off. Maybe if my life depended on it I could even poke around and find it. The general place, anyway, maybe not the exact spot. But only if I was out there, you know?"

"Okay then," I say. "Let's go."

He looks at me blankly for a second. "You're kidding."

"Not at all."

"I'm a dying guy here."

"If you were willing to let me strangle you to death, you can hardly argue with me taking you for a ride. The ride is much less likely to be fatal."

"Except my daughter'll kill me."

"Okay, fine," I say. "We'll go with the strangulation."

"Get my coat out of the closet," Chet says.

★  ★  ★

We've been cruising around out here in the mountains for more than two hours now, Chet's wheelchair in the backseat. Chet chewing on his nails even though there's nothing left to chew on, really. Half the time on roads that may not even be roads. More like fire roads or something.

The sky is heavy and dark, like it wants to rain again. It's close to the same time of year that Pearl disappeared. We're coming up on an anniversary shortly.

"What do you think?" I say. I'm starting to get impatient. I'm starting to feel like we've covered the same territory more than once.

"Must be further up," he says. He sounds distracted. "Unless we passed it already."

I slam on the brakes and skid a few feet in the dirt. Chet flies forward against the restraints of his seat belt like a sock doll.

"You're not really going to help me here, are you, Chet?"

He looks in my direction but not into my eyes. Then away again, out the window, to the same mountain scenery we've been seeing for hours. Rocks and scrubby trees. "No, I'm trying, really."

But I know he's lying from the way he avoids my eyes.

I sigh and rub my eyes and sit back with my eyes closed, admitting defeat. Knowing he came out here to get me off his back, not to help me. Not to give me what I need. I have the picture of my father in my shirt pocket. I can feel the stiffness of it. I try to focus on that instead. But two parents doesn't seem like asking too much. Especially since they're both long dead.

"I have to get out," Chet says. He's talking like a kindergartner asking to go to the boys' room. "I have to have a smoke."

"Bullshit. You're already dying from that crap. Why do you need to keep doing it?"

"You never smoked, huh? I can tell. Please. Really. It's important."

I sigh again. Then I get out and pull his wheelchair out of the back of my car. Unfold it and bring it around to the passenger side. Help him out. Help him fall into it. He falls heavily for a man who weighs near nothing at all.

I lean on the car, and he takes a pack out of his coat pocket and lights up. Pulls a deep hit. When he releases it, a cloud of smoke flies in my direction and I wave it away again. Go around him to stand on the upwind side. We look out over the valley together for a long time.

"It's gonna be real hard on my family," he says. "When all this hits the fan."

"I'm not sure what you're talking about, Chet."

"You know," he says. "Sure you know."

I don't argue with him. I wonder if he's fully cognizant. If he's in his right mind.

"I have to pee," he says.

"Okay, fine. Go pee."

"Not that easy. You gotta help me."

"You're not serious, right?"

"No, I mean it. I can't get my chair over those rocks. At least help me get behind that scrub. Some kind of privacy."

"Chet, there's no one within ten miles of here. I'll look the other way."

"A man's got his dignity," he says. He sounds like he's crying, or just at the edge of it. He swipes at his nose with the back of his coat sleeve.

So I wheel his chair over the rocks and around the scrub.

"Help me stand up," he says.

"Oh hell, Chet, can't you just sort of turn sideways?"

"I'll piss all over myself if I try. Come on. Just do this one thing."

I lift him out of the chair and we stand together; I'm holding him up with one arm around his shoulder. I look the other way, off toward the valley. Watch the storm clouds piling up. Thinking they look the way I feel. Dark and building.

Then I wheel him back to the car. Pile him in.

"Okay," I say. "I give up. I'll take you back."

And I turn the car around on that tight little unpaved road and head back.

Three, four, five miles later, he shouts out, startling me.

"Stop right here!"

I slam on the brakes, and we sit there a moment in silence.

"Is this the spot?" I ask.

"Pretty close to it, yeah."

"Did you know that on the way out?"

"Yeah."

I pull on the hand brake and shut down the engine.

"I'm sorry," he says. "It's just that I know you're gonna go straight to the authorities with this, and they'll dig up this whole damn mountainside, and I was just thinking how awful this is gonna be for my kids, even if I'm already gone."

I breathe a minute and then say, "I wasn't actually planning to try to dig her up."

"Oh," he says. "You weren't?"

"I wasn't thinking that way, no."

"Okay. Why then? I mean, why not?"

I'm not sure how to explain. Should I tell him how I feel about the thought of a backhoe or even a handheld shovel slicing through the tiny vertebrae of her neck or spine? Or just try to explain that the body is not the heart of the issue here? That it's more about a reverence for the last place on earth visited by her soul. About my wanting to visit that place, too.

About marking the spot.

But it's all hazy and hard to pin down, so I just say, "I'm not sure how to explain."

"Get the chair," he says. "I'll show you as best I can."

I wheel him as far as possible across the rocks, but the chair gets hung up over and over, and it's getting hard on both of us. Finally I lift him up onto my back and carry

CATHERINE RYAN HYDE

him piggyback. Every now and then one bony hand appears beside my head, pointing the way. I feel as if I'm in the presence of ghosts. Plural.

"Stop here," he says after a mile or so.

I set him down, and he folds onto himself in the dirt. Looks around.

"It's either the side of this hill or the side of that one," he says. "I'm not jacking you around. I'm really trying. But things change, you know? Erosion, and trees fall down, and things don't look just exactly the same. But if you're not really digging, just wanting to see the place, it's right around here somewhere. Over there or over there. I'm sorry I can't say closer than that. I really tried."

"I know," I say. "It's okay."

I look around and breathe. Memorize the site in every possible way, so I can always find it again. Much the way I'm sure Chet did that night. I raise my face to the wind and feel for signs of Pearl around here somewhere, but there's no one here but us. I'm sure he's right—I believe this is the right place. But it's been washed clean now. The past has moved aside.

"You know," Chet says, "that thing you said about how if you knew everything about somebody, then you'd understand? I think that might be true of everything. Everybody. I think if you walked every minute of somebody's life in his shoes then everything he did would make sense to you, even the bad things. That's why I left the force. Went out on a stress pension. When you stop seeing differences between them and you, you gotta quit and go home."

I pick him up onto my back, and we begin the long walk to the car.

By the time we get to his house, he's out cold. Head back on the seat, mouth open. Worn down from the trip, I suppose.

I pull up in front of his house and I'm struck with an awful thought. I pick up one of his wrists and feel around for a pulse. I'm not sure what I feel or if I feel anything at all, and my gut turns icy and tingly. But after a second I find it. A pulse. Weak, but there. I beep my horn lightly, and his daughter comes out and takes over. Opens out the wheelchair, lifts him back in. He never wakes up.

She turns a horrible look in my direction. Holds a hand in front of his nose feeling for breath. I can tell when she gets it. When she realizes he's just sleeping. The look softens, and she turns her eyes on me in a whole different way.

"Get what you wanted?" she asks.

"Yeah," I say. "I think so. I'm not really sure what I wanted. But I got something."



While I'm driving back up the coast I look at my watch. I'll be about ten minutes late to pick up the kids at school. So I step on it, hoping to get back some of that time. My wife is home with the new baby, and besides, we have only the one car. They'll wait for me. They're good kids. They know I wouldn't leave them waiting long.

I wonder if I should tell them what I learned today. Mitchell is at that age where he jumps from the middle of the room all the way onto his bed and pretends it's just a game. Says he does it for no reason in particular. He doesn't know he didn't invent the fear of something under the bed. That it didn't start with him.

Pearl still every now and then crawls into bed with us, claiming a bad dream. We all have these bogeymen, from the time we're old enough to reason, they just don't have any faces or names. We're all scared of something but we can't quite put our finger on what. Today I looked over my shoulder and saw mine. Memorized faces and took names.

What I can't figure out is whether I should be comforted or terrified by what I discovered. There is no bogeyman. Just a bunch of flawed humans, some more flawed than others, but more or less cut from the same human mold.

## MITCH, *age 50:* **the marker**

It's raining on the top of this mountain. We're huddled up here in a tent, hoping it will pass. It's dark, and a little windy. I wanted to put off this trip until after the storm, but it's an anniversary of sorts. It's the day Pearl left Leonard at my house and disappeared, with twenty-five years added on.

And it's the rainy season, just like it was then.

I was thinking maybe leave the kids at home, but Leonard promised, and he hates to break a promise to them. Or to anybody else, for that matter. And a different night was out of the question. He didn't say it was because of the significance of the date. He didn't have to. Some things are just there, and anybody with eyes can see them.

All he said was, "Worst that can happen, they'll get wet."

And it's true, really. Why does the rain trouble me

more in a tent than it would in a house? I can't even say.

So I called in sick at school, they called up a substitute teacher, and here we are.

Mitchy is out like a light but Pearl is sitting up with us, in the light of the lantern, leaning against Leonard's side.

Now and then she looks up and watches shadows flicker across the inside dome of the tent. You can see her listening, hearing the wind buffet the fabric in irregular gusts. It's just that right amount of fear. Just enough for a kid to handle, providing some part of the kid is in direct contact with some part of the parent.

"I was just thinking," Leonard says. "I was just thinking how close I came to missing all this."

"That crossed my mind, too," I say.

He looks down at Pearl, who looks up into his eyes to see what she's done right all of a sudden.

He cups her chin in one of his hands. "I mean, not only would I not have gotten a chance to see this face, but nobody else in the world would have, either."

Pearl makes a face. Crosses her eyes and sticks her tongue out. A way of diffusing the compliment.

"I stand corrected," Leonard says. "The world might've gotten by."

★ ★ ★

After Pearl is asleep, her back up against her brother, I ask Leonard a question I've been meaning to ask.

"Did you want to hurt him? Maybe just some part of you? Some little instinct out for revenge? Or maybe just justice?"

I ask because in the past I've noticed things I thought were missing in Leonard, but they were only delayed.

We sit still and listen to the rain hammer on the fabric of the tent dome. We're still dry in here, though.

"That's what got Pearl. Somebody out for justice."

"That might not stop you from wanting to, though."

"I didn't. I didn't want to. I thought I would. But it just wasn't there."

"What if you had met the other guy?"

"I don't know. But I don't think so."

"He killed your mother."

"Yeah, and my mother killed my father," he says. "And I still have to believe that she had her reasons. How can I hate the guy who killed my mother without hating the woman who killed my father? It's almost exactly the same crime."

I lie down. In time Leonard does the same. Our hands are clasped behind our heads.

Leonard says, "Leonard Devereaux Kowalski Sung Di-Mitri. And to think I started life as the boy with no last name."

"And I was so excited when I found one for you."

"Well, back then it was a pretty big deal. I mean, it

seemed like an issue. I took it hard. I thought I didn't belong anywhere. Never occurred to me it would turn out I belong a lot of different places at once. All over the place. Right now I belong right here. On this mountain. Thanks for coming up here with me, Mitch."

After ten or fifteen minutes goes by, I look over and see that he's fallen asleep. His face looks young in the soft lantern light. More the way I knew him as a boy. Another one of those faces the world would have been poorer without.

I blow out the lantern and try to get some sleep myself.

When I wake up it's nearly light, and the rain has stopped. The children are asleep beside me, but not Leonard.

I open the tent flap.

He's about a hundred feet away, standing on a slope of tumbled rocks, facing away from me. His shirt is off, and he's standing out in the cold in nothing but his jeans, his arms straight out from his sides, the tattoo visible even from here. There's a mist, a sort of wet, heavy fog hanging over the mountain, and Leonard is standing on the approximate site of his mother's grave, and he is a cross.

I watch in silence, knowing how little I understood until just now.

Leonard was never trying to be a Christ. He was trying to be a marker. He used the tattoo to transform himself into the only tangible proof that Pearl had lived and then died. He was her grave marker when she had no grave to mark.

And now he's finally found where to stand.

I watch him for the longest time.

I want to walk up behind him and throw my arms around his back, but I don't want to disturb his delicate balance.

I want to remind him—and myself—of the first time he showed me the tattoo. Standing in Jake and Mona's garage in a beam of sun from the skylight, under the bare wings of his glider in progress. He told me he wasn't going to live to be thirty.

But he is thirty. Right now.

And I don't even have to ask if he regrets the tattoo, because I already know.

After I've watched long enough, I hike out to the car and get the camp stove. So I can stoke it up and get some coffee going. Maybe breakfast for the kids.

When I get back, the kids are awake. They've found their own way to their father, and they're standing with him, still in their sleepers on the wet, muddy ground, each kid hugging one of his legs.

So I decide that if they can do it without disturbing him, maybe I can, too.

I think about Pearl, and how everything she did, whether it was right or wrong, caused Leonard's life to intersect with mine the way it did. If she had done anything differently, not only would I not have had him but I wouldn't have had my grandkids, either. And I think how much poorer I would have been without him, without all of them.

Without all the things I've learned.

Then I walk quietly up behind him and wrap my arms around him from behind, and he comes out of his marker position, his cross, and wraps his arms around my arms. I hope I didn't make him stop before he was done.

But that's silly, I think. How could he stop before he was done? If he stopped, he was done.

I silently congratulate him on being done, and he pats my arm.

I think he hears and understands most of what I don't say to him.

I think he always has.

**THE END**

# Pay It Forward
## Catherine Ryan Hyde

---

It all started with the social studies teacher's extra-credit project:

*Think of an idea for world change, and put it into action*

Whilst this proved a little ambitious for most of his classmates, twelve-year-old Trevor thought he would start by doing something good for three people. But instead of paying *him* back, he would ask them to 'pay it forward' by doing a favour for three more people. If it all went to plan, Trevor thought, it would be the start of a long chain of human kindness . . .

Sound unlikely? Well a lot of other people had their doubts too – Trevor's teacher, his classmates, his mother, in fact everyone in his small California town. It could never really work . . . could it?

'HYDE'S BOOK DELIVERS A PROFOUND VISION: THE SIMPLE MAGIC OF THE HUMAN HEART'
*SAN FRANCISCO CHRONICLE*

HAVE YOU HEARD?
www.payitforwardmovement.org
www.payitforwardfoundation.org

9780552774253

# Second Hand Heart
## Catherine Ryan Hyde

*She's been given a chance to live.*
*But does she know how?*

## One girl
Vida is nineteen, very ill, and has spent her short life preparing for her death. But a new chance brings its own story, because for Vida to live, someone had to die.

## One man
Richard has just lost his beloved wife in a car accident. He hasn't even begun to address his grief, but feels compelled to meet the girl who inherited his wife's heart.

## Someone else's heart
In hospital Vida sees Richard and immediately falls in love. Of course he dismisses her as a foolish child. But is she? Can two people be bound by a second hand heart?

9780552776622